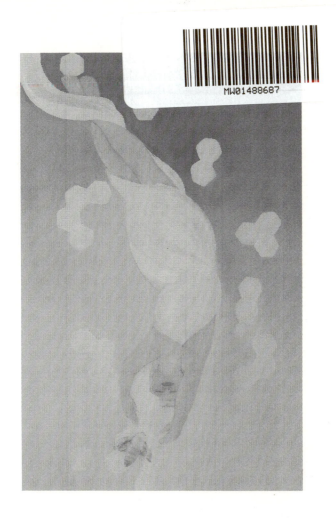

DANCING WITH A THOUSAND BEES

By Karrie Marie Baxley

APIS MELLIFERA

The Honeybee
Is
145 Million Years Old!

There are special moments, hours, or even days, that seep into our being and change our reality from the ordinary to the extraordinary. These glimpses can lead us into a space of grandeur and are understood through our heart.

Sometimes, this becomes a catalyst where we are captured by a flutter deep inside that ignites the imagination and world around us. These moments reveal possibilities of wonder and open doorways to a new sense of seeing.

This story is about the non ordinary and ordinary coming together. This is a story of a fluttering heart.

The Dance of a Thousand Bees

The soft constant vibration
Awakening and enticing me within
My head begins to feel a lilt
As the powerful dance begins

Floating into a lofty space
Above the ground below
My body is filled with rapture
From the buzz, the hum, the glow

The space is intoxicating
A scent of honey fills the air
A scent in the winds talking to the bees
As they all dance so near

The ancient goddess playing
With the flowers, gardens, and trees
Becoming one as she suckles
Tell me what does she see?
A hundred violet colors shooting in the air
Calling to the sweet goddess
Please, love, come here.

By Karrie Marie Baxley

With Love
To the Sweet Honeybee

And my beloveds Daniel, Kevin-Anne, Sean Patrick, and Michael Kian who have filled me with love, joy, awe, and pure wonder.

A Great thanks to my family, who has always given me love and support. Heartfelt thanks to my beloved community; how sweet is the nectar of our communal hearts.

And thanks to my dear friend Maril, for helping me bring this love to completion.

Contents

The ancient honeybee is one of nature's masterful feminine wonders. She brings many parts of our world together to create a cohesive whole—with honey, mead, and many healing gifts. Through my experience in taking care of honeybees I have found myself in awe as they create entire worlds before me. As I listen I hear a little bee trying to be heard as it delicately pollinates our world, creating sustenance for everything it touches. Honeybees have existed in the fields and forests across the planet before the beginning of humanity's time on earth. Today the honeybee is imperative to the survival of humanity.

This is a story about a honeybee, a woman, and magic from a beautiful creature in peril. Through my first season as a beekeeper in the countryside of the Midwest I became enchanted with this little creature. Soon, I began journaling about my experiences, feelings and glimpses with the bees and cosmic ecstasy began to unfold before me. I have found a great female communion with the bee that is awakening old forgotten feelings within me along with experiencing an inquisitive joy. It is awakening a beautiful dance deep inside.

This journey has shown me how indescribably important the honeybee is to the survival of humanity. As the bee creates from a multitude of things, this book presents a multitude of arts to tell its story. Woven together with visual arts, poetry, and prose to bring light and beauty to this majestic creature.

To speak truly, few adult persons can see nature.
Most persons do not see the sun.
At least they have a very superficial seeing.
The sun illuminates only the eye of the man,
but shines into the eye and the heart of the child.
The lover of nature is he whose inward and outward
senses are still truly adjusted to each other;
who has retained the spirit of infancy even into the
era of manhood.

Ralph Waldo Emerson
1803–1882

May we all see nature in the spirit of infancy!

One

Someone's Knocking on My Door

SUMMERTIME

**And harmonies unheard in sound create the harmonies
we hear
And wake the soul to the consciousness of beauty.**

**Plotinus
204–270 CE**

The honeybee is echoing in my mind much like a knocking on my door that just won't stop as I marvel at the majestic
sight. Here in the countryside is a flurry of life playing across the
land. As I watch the display of creatures around me I yearn for
little honeybees to come and join this lively affair. Honeybees
flutter much like the glistening stars in the heavens, except that
these creatures are earthbound.

I have been dreaming of bees for years now. I have thought about what led me to become a beekeeper, and the truth is that many reasons have brought me to this new space among the bees. I am in a new juncture in my life as I move from the city to the countryside with a new marriage and teenage boys. We moved from the center of Kansas City to Gardner, Kansas. I have dreamed of a space among nature to understand my place in the scheme of things. With a love of flowers and gardening I began creating beds around our home.

I find in understanding the natural world there are imperative basic needs. First, space is needed along with a healthy environment, water and nutrients and then everything grows. At least I thought it was that simple, yet our world is complicated now and many of our species are struggling. The flowers and vegetable gardens are dependent on rich soils and pollinators for blossoms and that requires bees. I wanted the gardens to be a micro-macro environment that enriched each other. In this recipe for communion the bee along with many other creatures are a prerequisite for growth. I also simply love bees and wanted to experience them in a very intimate way. Perhaps they were calling to me as much as I was calling to them.

Moving to nature is a new experience for my entire family, and quite a large change from our norm. My two sons, daughter and myself have always lived in the middle of the city and loved it. My daughter had moved to her own place in the city. Luckily, my husband lived in the country for years. He had the equipment and knowlege to care for ten acres of land. Not only was the terrain different the sounds are different. In the city there is a comfortable breath that hums with familiarity. In the city I am surrounded with many things I love being close to: the galleries, museums, music, dining, and the activity. The city is comfortable and imbues me with an energetic ambience that enlivens my senses.

Yet I find myself longing for a connection to nature and a different type of noise, a different energetic ambience. I want room; I want a lot of room. It feels as if the wild unknown is beckoning me with an enticing call. Perhaps this is when the honeybees first began calling me. Daniel, my husband, my two teenage sons, Sean and Michael, and two basset hounds, bound to this new space in the country. It is our new place among the wild, where Sean, Michael, and I are like deer in the headlights!

This Wild Place of Lions, Tigers, and Bears. Oh My!

Well, there aren't really lions, tigers, and bears out here in the countryside of Kansas. Though where we live is wild and natural, and things are definitely untamed. There is a stark contrast between living with the sounds and activity of a city and the sounds and activity of the wilderness. They are both quite powerful and echo in the heart, yet carry different vibrations. The sounds in the belly of the city are exciting, loud, and busy. The noises in the country are exciting, but not made from humans at all. There are no sirens, cars, or neighbors' noises out here. In the belly of the wild, there is a play between silent stillness and loud, wild chaos.

Nestled in the wilderness is our home, which resembles an old farmhouse. It has a wraparound porch that provides great views of incoming storms, cloudscapes, and the setting sun, as it laces the horizon with beautiful displays of color. The view takes my breath away, with its vast expanse of nature as far as I can see. I was used to looking up into trees, but the sky was filled with lights, not stars, in the city. Now when I look up into the sky I see a million stars, darkness, and no distractions.

Several years ago I turned toward nature, seeking a teacher from the natural world, and now that teacher has appeared as a honeybee. I have been having dreams of bees for over a year. During this time I have experienced many odd coincidences, a friend of mine went to spend a summer at a bee farm with a shaman in Europe, coming home with great stories and experiences. Then bees just began appearing everywhere for me, bees would land on me at restaurants, or appear at unusual places like parking lots or inside a friends car. I begin reading books about bees and beekeeping and each experience entices me to want to learn more. I am becoming passionate about the bees and for Christmas my husband gifted me a beehive. I am now not just talking, or reading about the bees I am ready to become a beekeeper. I feel like I am in a world of bees.

I search for bees in the beds of flowers that stretch around our home much like a well-nourished wreath. Tons of little creatures play among the beds and rise up in a giddy display, yet there are no honeybees in my gardens.

The flower and vegetable gardens on our land are organic and I am continually learning about the interdependence of our natural world: what is needed and what is not. The honeybee is needed! I find that what I mix into the land affects everything around it in an intimate way. I am now caretaking with my mind present to all the living entities lying beneath my feet and I want them to thrive. I also want the honeybee in my gardens.

Soon, through my trials and errors with nature, I begin feeling a deep connection to her, much like an extension of my body. As time progresses this connection grows, and I find myself spending more and more time outside. A lovely desire intensifies within me to be connected with the natural world. I soon plant an assortment of goodies to provide a great supply of food for the creatures around the gardens. I entice many bumblebees and other great insects by planting butterfly bushes, bee balm, roses, and an assortment of flowers, yet the honeybee is not among them.

The woods and creatures in the countryside provide a display of natural beauty, and one of these creatures is in trouble. The news about the honeybees is a story of nature in peril. There is much talk about this creature and my thoughts about the honeybee continue to grow. As the gardens grow the number of insects around my flowers and vegetable gardens grow as well and I become aware of the importance of balance. Soon my gardens begin to fill with a beautiful assortment of blossoms and as time passes the bees become ever so loud, but only in my mind.

I watch the bumblebees, butterflies, hummingbirds, and songbirds playing in delight and I am taken aback by the universes that exist right here in front of me. Their sound feels like a beautiful gala, where everything is a heavenly dance of delight. It feels like nature is paying me a visit—or at least letting me watch an enchantment. Soon what I am seeing begins to change, subtly at first, and yet my vision is definitely changing. It reminds me of my first semester at art school and we were working only in charcoals for months, after a while everything appeared to me only in black and white, as my eyes were cueing in on subtle differences around me. Now in intimate communion with the bees my eyesight is changing as if the colors in nature are alive and glowing, and everything in the garden is dancing.

This new garden of bees will be found at the back of our house by following a crooked path into the woods. Once you reach the woods, two large thorn trees flank each side of the path, marking the entrance to the honeybees' garden. The bee-hives will sit nestled in a circle of trees, with deep, thick woods at their back. The woods lie to the north and east of our home, and a large pond sits at the southeast corner of the honeybees' garden. Wildflowers and swaying grasses dapple the landscape everywhere you look.

BEES BEES BEES BEES BEES BEES BEES

This Goddess has been calling in my ear, first lightly,
And as time has moved on, the call has become a siren.

When we hear a calling,
Do we simply hear the murmur?
Or
Begin to move toward the calling?

My knowledge of honeybees is very limited, so I begin my inquiries about beekeeping. I read magazines on bees, books of bees and how to books on beekeeping. There are reported cases of 30–70 percent of hives lost due to colony collapse disorder, also called CCD, and this is a trend that has been going on for years. Cases of hives totally lost to this disease are becoming more and more common across the world. Yet this little bee is imperative for our survival. The honeybee is quite beautiful and tiny and it's hard to imagine its disappearance.

There are many theories regarding the cause of bee colony decline and how to alleviate the problem. All the theories are connected including, the use of chemicals, disease, the clearing of land, and other practices that affect our environment. The problem is believed to be a type of cocktail that has been created and not a disease at all. Instead, it is thought to be the phenomenon of many factors coming together with unhealthy predicaments for the honeybee. All of these components are increasing like a snowball falling down a mountain, and the ball gets bigger and bigger as it falls.

The grand display of natural beauty is an interrelated dynamic of everything working together and dependent on its pollinators. The honeybee is one of our most important pollinators on Earth. Albert Einstein is credited with saying, "You can't solve a problem with the same thinking that created it." Nor can you solve a problem by doing nothing. There are many scientists who believe that without honeybees, mankind would starve in four years. This is a powerful impact that these little creatures have on our world and the consequences of their demise would affect all of humanity.

The honeybees have lived on earth for over 145 million years. The first evidence of their appearance dates back to the Cretaceous Period, when dinosaurs roamed earth. During the Cretaceous Period the lands were pristine and the honeybees began thriving on earth for millions of years. Our land in the country has been left for nature and not touched by humans for decades. This is not the same as pristine yet it has been left alone for nature to play with. Throughout the ages many of our historical figures have kept honeybees such as Thomas Edison,

Ben Franklin, Thomas Jefferson, and Shakespeare, who all cared for the balance of nature. In the world today people such as, Martha Stewart, Oprah Winfrey and President Barack and First Lady Michelle Obama are beekeepers to name a few.

I have fond childhood memories of playing with bees that evoke a sense of gaiety and a childlike innocence. Honeybees bring back memories of flowers and laughter, playful ease, and delightful carefree summer days. I have always liked bees.

As time progresses my desire to care for the bees begins to stir. Now, at this time of my life when my children are leaving the nest and I am in my fifties I have been in the process of letting go, and the idea of caretaking anything seems remote. Yet the thought of working with the honeybee is intriguing me and has taken ahold of me. I have no clue what that entails, if they are hard or easy to work with, or if it is even possible. Yet the honeybees are calling me and I am listening.

As I listen to the sounds of the coyote and other wild animals at night, I feel a deep connection and love for this space in the wild. In nature as in all of life, there is always movement. Nothing is idle and nature is a great teacher of perpetual motion and constant change. Here everything is so alive, as the individual hearts beat together and a rhythm echoes across the land. Here is where the orchestra of nature can be heard, with all of her children singing in a beautiful communal song. It soothes my heart to sit and listen to her symphony.

As I sit in this natural wonderland in the country, with the animals of the wild all around, their sounds are intimate and personal and I listen contently. After living with the noises of the city, the noises of the country continually take me by surprise. I had the idea that living in the country would be quiet, still and calming. To my surprise, it is a strong, powerful sound when all the nocturnal creatures begin moving on the land. The deer prance around our home as I run from window to window to watch these magnificent creatures. Then there are gangs of coyotes, howling around our home and at the edge of the woods. There are usually two or more gangs of coyotes howling to one another. As they all begin to sing, the dark land fills with a new noise—a noise of nature, not man.

On our farm in the countryside, I am aware that this is nature's space, not the space of humans. It is thick with the rich essence of the wild and in this space the language of humanity does not dominate. The longer I am on the land and in the woods I find myself walking differently and listening differently. I am learning a new language. I am learning the language of nature.

Language is the system humans have created in order to communicate with one another, and there are hundreds of languages. But the ability to communicate is not just humanity's gift; everything in nature has the ability to communicate. Everything has a language, whether we hear or understand it or not, and in nature the system of communication is different. Many of the creatures on earth use a tone that is inaudible to the human ear, yet they communicate magnificently.

It is said that elephants continue to vocalize at night at a level that is inaudible to us, yet they still communicate with one another. There is a beautiful story of a man who had worked and lived in Africa with the elephants most of his life. When he died, elephants from miles and days away traveled to his home. They used their trunks to interlock and formed a procession to where he lay. It's said they stayed overnight, moaning and communing with one another, and then began their procession home. The question is how did the elephants know of his death? We do know they were in mourning for someone they loved, and communicated in a language we are unaware of.

To communicate with nature and understand the secrets of the universe, we need to understand how the universe speaks. There is a wise saying in regards to secrets in the universe, it says nature keeps no secrets, she answers all questions in her own language. To understand the answer, you must understand the language.

The language of nature requires me to be conscious and aware as I walk gently in order to hear her. Soon a wonderful calming seeps into my senses as if I am being soothed or lulled by something enormous, perhaps Mother Earth herself. As time goes by and my connection with this wild space changes, I am finding nature and myself are one. We are intertwined and dependent on one another.

The interdependence among creatures of the natural world began to unfold to me, and I was reminded of the movie with Kevin Costner, Field of Dreams where they say something to the affect: if you build it, they will come. I realized that the natural world shows up if you provide a space for it and I had the space. The balance of space for everything in nature is in honoring everything as having a place, to coexist together. The balance of nature is like a circle. It is a continual sustenance for everything involved, as the circle continues to spin and feed upon itself; everything in it is nurtured. This balance of nature speaks to a natural rhythm of the universe, and to the coexistence in nature that creates indescribable beauty.

As the bounty of springtime arrives, the news continues of bees dying at alarming rates across the United States and other countries. Over the last three years we have lost 30 percent or more of our bees in the United States. The bees are beginning a conversation with me and they are becoming very loud!

Our land is nestled in the outskirts of Kansas City, surrounded by large wooded areas, fields, creeks and lots of water. Water is essential for bees, as with all living creatures. A large creek called Kill Creek runs behind our property, giving an ample supply of fresh water for the natural world. The diversity of land, food, and resources gives home to a wide variety of living creatures. At times I feel as if I am residing in the middle of a wildlife zoo.

One of the creatures of the wild was murmuring intently in my ear, perhaps wishing to join the zoo. The idea buzzed around my head for months and I knew the buzzing would not stop until I actually did something about it. The bees were calling me with a sweet constant hum and I could no longer ignore their call.

Two

The Color of Bees

MARCH

Let us turn elsewhere, to the wasps and bees,
Which unquestionable come first in the laying up of a
heritage
for their offspring

Jean Henri Fabri
1823–1915

   A deep sensual connection with the bee is stirring within me and a strong arousal of my senses awakens fond memories of my childhood. They come flooding back, much like moments triggered by the scent of something familiar from long ago. My memories take me back to a beekeeper that lived around the corner from my childhood home:
   I was about five years old and life was simple, easy and happy. The beekeeper would let me sit and watch him work with his bees. Thousands of honeybees flew everywhere around him,

as if they were having their own wonderful dance or gala. This was not a dance of fear or aggression instead it was a dance of love between the beekeeper and the bees. The bees were not attacking him. They were communing with him and I was entranced. It felt as if he was in an altered state when I watched him and his bees, as if he was in another world.

The beekeeper would walk gently over to me, as if he were gliding a few feet off the ground, and hand me a honeycomb to suck on. I would sit there watching in delight—the glimmer in the beekeepers eyes, the dance of the bees, and the plush, beautiful gardens. As I sat sucking on the honeycomb I would listen to the soft constant hum of the bees. This was a magical moment of absolute peace, awe, and wonder. This is a moment I remember to this day. It is a memory I can even smell.

Now, I listen to the sounds echoing across the land and remember the feelings of joy from my childhood memories, and then I take a view. I view everything from that feeling of joy in my childhood with the scent of blackberries, soft breezes against my skin and total contentment.

I view the horizon at that majestic
time—the in-between time
When the sky is hazed in blue and everything shifts
And the grand old trees straighten their backs as the
angels land on their limbs
Water drips from the heavens into the springs
Then somehow I know I am the water, I am the wind
I am the tree swaying in the heavens and I am the echo
traveling through the woods

I stop and hold my breath to remember this moment
The moment when all of nature dances
together, myself included
The coming together
Here is where the divine has pierced my heart
and I am everything
And I am nothing
As I try to hold onto this moment before
it flows through my fingers
And out of my grasp.

Nature has a way of taking my breath away with her beauty. I soon begin talking to others who have similar interests in honeybees. My curiosity is heightened about the honeybees and I want to learn more for many reasons: their importance for pollination, to help the honeybee, and to experience that feeling of ecstasy from my childhood.

There are many avenues to learn about honeybees and learning from a beekeeper in your area is a good way to start. It's also useful for any future endeavors! There are beekeeping organizations, events and gatherings as well as courses that are presented either from existing beekeepers or at community colleges. This lead me to two courses at our community college called Intro to Beekeeping and Beekeeping 101.

I sign up for the courses at our Community College for Beekeeping and to try to get a hold on what being a beekeeper actually means. The first class is intro into bee keeping and made up of a range of people from young to old, each with different reasons to be here. A woman named Beth sits down beside me, and we share a large lab table. We are both clueless about the bees and also both excited to learn. Beth is writing an exposé about bees for a community newspaper, and I am preparing for bees at my home.

A local beekeeper named Bob is the caretaker for the honeybees on the campus and is teaching the class. Bob began taking care of honeybees when he was fourteen and now is a beekeeper and educator at the College. He comes with a lot of exuberance and an obvious love for honeybees as well as a wealth of knowledge. The first class is taken up with handouts and basic information about the honeybee. Most of my classmates and I are amazed from the beginning. The presentation lit me up from inside.

After the first class I was hooked and wanted more information. The next several classes were more hands-on, as honeycombs, honeybee tools, and accessories were passed through the class. Next we got to peer through parts of the hive that was brought for our viewing, and begin to understand the colony life, or life of bees. Beth is enjoying the class as much as I am and the awesomeness of the honeybee amazes both of us. As we both write feverishly, we find ourselves writing about the female. As Beth's writes her paper and I fill my notepads we are both becoming passionate and wanting to know more.

After the first series of classes I feel as if I have been given a little bite of something that tastes wonderful! I sign up for Beekeeper 101, and so does Beth along with many of the people from the introductory class. We sign up for our beekeeper suits to wear at our first visit to the honeybees' hives for the next class.

At the second class, Bob instructs us on visiting the beehives while we put on our suits. I am excited to actually see the beehive with the class. The beekeeper's suits are not easy to put on. First, the netted hat needs to be attached to the bodysuit, which is tricky. We each need assistance to get the suits, hats, and gloves on. Luckily, Bob has brought in three other beekeepers to help us get dressed and each one of use needs assistance in some way. The suits are all white and cover our body entirely with a netted hat that zips onto the jumpsuit and long elbow length gloves. Once we are all dressed and prepared, we head from the classroom to the woods on campus.

Now, we are all dressed in beekeeper's suits and our sight is greatly diminished by the netted veil. Beth and I hold hands as we descend three flights of stairs to the door leading outside. We are clumsy and giddy as we walk through the parking lot and into the woods, flanked by Bob, the other beekeepers, and our classmates.

Once we are close to the pathway leading to the hives we are asked to quiet ourselves and remain calm. Soon we see over twelve hives in the distance, sitting deep within the woods. One of the beekeepers goes ahead of us and begins to smoke around one of the hives we are approaching. Smoking is used frequently with beekeeping. A small smoker is filled with twine, twigs and paper and then lit. Once the smoker is lit, white smoke billows out directed towards the hives. The intention of smoking is to keep the bees busy and calm. Some beekeepers will put lavender or other herbs inside the smoker to help calm the bees for a while. Bob is quite happy and exuberant around the beehives, and we are invited to circle around the hive they have smoked and are ready to open. Two other beekeepers, Rick and Jim, begin to lift up the lid of the hive. As the lid opens they place it on the ground and hundreds of bees ascend around us.

Honeybees fly chaotically around all of us in the class and we experience the bees for the first time. They dart from one direction to the next with the speed and skill of a racetrack driver, except they are not limited by an oval. While the bees are flying around they begin to bat at us and I quickly understand the need for a beekeeping suit. There are so many bees that my vision is now greatly limited. Honeybees like to head for the head, eyes, ears, and nose and they will continue to attack again and again. Once they get their groove of attack many other bees will join in and soon the netted veil is covered with bees trying to get inside.

Then, Bob takes out several slats from the hive itself. Each slat is covered with bees, honey, and honeycombs, and Bob hands us the slats. I take hold of the wooden slat by holding the edges, and carefully view the comb. There are hundreds of bees walking around, clumped together on the slat, and flying everywhere around us. Five or six slats from the hive are removed for us to view and pass around. As each slat is removed from the hive, more and more bees rise into the air.

After we have viewed the hive for a time, the slats are put back and Bob puts on the lid so the bees can calm down and go back into their home. The class proceeds to another hive. At each hive we are shown how to smoke the hive, open the lid, and retrieve the slats from the hive. Every hive is different in the production and the size of the colony, and we are able to see the differences while listening to our instructors. After we have opened five hives there are thousands of bees in flight around us. Bob and the other beekeepers love it, while many of us from the class are in hesitant awe.

I feel scared and excited all at the same time. There is a flutter happening inside me and I am very aware of the power of thousands of bees, they can be content and create wonder or they can attack and scare the hell out of me. One of the girls in front of me sits on some honey and as she stands up hundreds of bees land on her bottom. We all stop and stare in astonishment, not knowing what to do. The bees descend on her in seconds, as Bob strides over in a calm easy gait and gently brushes off the bees, and they all fly away.

I am astounded as I look inside the beehive and see a labyrinthine world. Thousands of bees fly feverishly around us to protect the hive, while the bees inside continue to work and protect their queen. Though I have hesitancy about the honeybees, I am also enthralled. Many of my fears about the honeybee seem to be unwarranted. As they fly chaotically around me I realize I love this feeling. The feeling of having hundreds of bees everywhere around me is wonderful. Now I have a great desire to begin the relationship with the bees.

When the beekeepers talk about their bees, their girls, their eyes light up. They all seem filled with a joy and lightness along with an intense love. They call them their girls with such a strong, deep, loving affection that it is uniquely enticing and contagious. Bob and the other beekeepers are all so happy being beekeepers and they have a strong relationship with the bees. At first I thought it a little odd, this intense affection, I mean, how can you have such an intimate relationship with a bee? After my first visit with the beehives, I understood a little of their affection.

The last remaining classes are spent with the hives. Each time we put on our beekeepers outfit and visit the hives, I feel an increasing familiarity or comfortableness with the bees. I find the queen bee through many examinations of the hive box—the queen never leaves the hive—and also feel comfortable working with the hives and the bees. During the last class everyone is given a complete guide to resources needed to begin beekeeping. The resources include contacts with local bee communities, bee magazines, information on how to take care of a hive and the contacts to buy everything required.

I put my desires into action and purchased the needed equipment to take care of two beehives from Bob. The beekeeper's advice is to always have a few hives at all times, since each queen is different in her productivity and lifespan. I know of two types of hives and go with one of each to get started. One of the hives is called a top-bar hive and the other is a traditional hive box. They each allow a different type of hive and comb production for the beekeeper and the honeybee.

Daniel surprised me with a top-bar hive for Christmas, which is a great gift and also encouragement from someone uncomfortable with bees. It is also my green light to begin this adventure.

The two types of hives are very different from one another in appearance and in the environment they create for a honeybee. The top-bar hive is a very natural way to collect honey, much like a honeybee creating her combs in a tree in the wild. The top-bar hive is low-impact, sustainable, and a natural way to keep bees. The hive is an elongated A-frame shaped wooden container. It rests upon wooden feet that keep the hive several feet above ground. Opening the top of the hive allows access to it. Inside, wooden bars are placed across the top of the A-frame. The bars are covered with a coat of beeswax on one side and then laid inside the top of the hive. They are arranged side by side, with a few inches between each bar for the bees to create

their combs. In this hive the bees create everything, from building the comb to creating the honey.

Picture of a Natural Heart-Shaped Honeycomb

Photography by Karrie Marie Baxley

When a honeybee creates a comb naturally she creates
a heart-shaped comb, and the beekeeper is gifted with the
whole heart honeycomb filled with honey. Now, how wonderful is that!

The heart honeycomb above is my first view of an actual comb created naturally. I have always had honeycombs from the traditional hive box. In a traditional hive box there are wooden slats with a comb texture that the bees create their honeycomb on. In a traditional hive you receive liquid honey, the honeybee uses the slat to help create the comb. In a top-bar hive the bee must create the comb entirely themselves. Therefore the only way to receive a heart-shaped comb is through the natural top-bar hive. I am amazed as I watch the honeybees in this hive and how beautiful this heart creation is. It is miraculous that, organically, a honeybee colony creates a heart.

The top-bar hive is thought to be the closest way a bee creates honey naturally and is effective, easy, and cost-efficient. This type of hive is used in many third-world countries, along with many beekeepers wanting the bee to exist in its most natural environment. The top-bar is limited by the size of the A-frame. Additional space cannot be added after the hive is full. Therefore, the hive's size needs to be monitored. If it gets too full the bees will swarm and leave.

The top-bar hive has a window on the side which allows me to observe the honeybees creating their honeycomb and honey without interruption to the colony inside. The honeybees are a marvel to watch.

Picture of Top-Bar Honeybee Hive
(Door on front allows viewing)

Photography by Karrie Marie Baxley

The other type of hive is a traditional box hive. This is the most common of beekeeper hives. The traditional boxes have slats that go inside the hive box with perforated combs already created on the slats, so the work of the bee is reduced when compared to the top-bar hive. In the traditional hive box the honey is created within the combs. The slats are placed inside the box and the bees create a wax comb on top of the slats and then fill the comb with honey. In this hive the bees do not have to spend energy creating the entire honeycomb. Consequently, more energy is spent on the honey process than the comb process. This is perhaps why the traditional hives are more popular. The traditional hive creates a lot more liquid honey than in the top-bar hive. In the top-bar hive, the importance is the creation of the heart honeycomb. Both types of hives create a delicious wonder—honey.

The traditional box hive has the advantage of being able to grow by placing more boxes on top of each other as the need arises. Delicious honey, liquid gold, is extracted from the slats within the boxes.

Picture of Traditional Beehive

Photography by Karrie Marie Baxley

As stated above, the work is decreased for the honeybee within the traditional hive box, since they do not have to create the entire comb from scratch.

I set up and prepared both honeybee hives at the edge of the woods, and I am ready for the bees. One way to set up a new hive (whether a top-bar or a traditional beehive) is by ordering a packaged set of honeybees. A set of bees contains the queen, her attendants and thousands of worker bees within a box, which is everything needed to start a hive. I ordered two complete packages of bees (Queen, and all) and anxiously waited for their arrival.

Each package of bees is held within a wire-cage box so the honeybees can breathe. The entire wooden box is approximately sixteen inches by ten inches with wire mesh around the entire box giving it an appearance of a cage. Within the large box is a smaller box that is approximately four inches by four inches holding the queen and her attendants. The Queens smaller caged box hangs inside the top of the larger box so all the other bees can smell her and is netted for air circulation. Bob had told me that once the bees arrive they need to be put into their hives in a timely manner and this means no delays, since they can get quite stirred up waiting for their home. Mail carriers also like to have them move on quickly. I suppose hearing thousands upon thousands of bees buzzing could be quite a play on the senses and very disturbing. The sound to me is constant and intoxicating.

The packages each come with seven to ten thousand bees, along with the queen bee. Within the box the queen's cage hangs separately, otherwise the other bees will swarm around the queen's cage, frantically trying to reach her. The queen is separated for her protection during time of travel, and because the queen and the colony of bees may be meeting for the first time. The colony can swarm or kill the queen if they don't know her or her pheromone scent. Therefore, a separation is given to allow time for communing with the queen. Her pheromone scent will connect the colony of bees as a family and they organically become one. I have placed the two hives in the southeast where the sun rises to greet the girls.

And now I wait.

Three

The Unveiling

MAY

Nature is the Art of God

Dante Alighieri
1452–1519

It is weeks and then months, and finally the bee packages arrive. I am excited to pick up the bees and quickly prepare the car, and my husband, for their arrival. When I pull into Bob's driveway I see over forty packages of honeybees in his garage. The sound is intense, overwhelming, and a little unsettling. I am so distracted by the presence of so many bees we need to step outside the garage to talk.

Bob goes over a quick refresher for installing the bees, along with some helpful tips and his phone number. We load the two boxes of honeybees into my SUV and off to home the bees and I go. As I close the car door I am instantly aware of the noise—the humming. The sound and the feeling of carrying fourteen thousand bees in my car is a bizarre and exciting feeling. I am aware of a hyped-up intensity building within my body. I can't wait to get home and work with these little creatures, and to get out of this enclosed space with them. My head is beginning to spin and I feel weirdly off-balance.

The noise of thousands of bees in my car for the thirty-minute drive is overpowering and at the same time hypnotic. They lull me into a trance with their melodic buzzing. Honeybees clump together and make a constant humming noise through the flapping of their wings. At first, the humming in the car is soft and gentle. I can barely hear them and it feels carefree and enjoyable. As we drive further, the sound level increases. The bees get excited, and I get excited right along with them. The intensity level within the car and my body rises. When the bees change their sounds my body reacts as well. Finally, we reach home and the entire car is buzzing so loudly that my senses are overtaken.

I can hear buzzing inside my head and I feel as though I'm in a bubble filled with this constant humming of bees. I step away from the car to get my bearings and find silence, yet wherever I stand, or however far I go from the car, the humming continues. Everything around me is a haze, and colors appear to be lighter. I continue to hear an echo, and the sound of the echo is somewhere inside my head now. I feel as if I have been hypnotized. The humming takes over much like water, in that it has totally taken over my body and is everywhere; there is even a palpitation with this noise of a bee, almost like a breath existing within the space of the hum.

I am doing this alone—no teachers present—and I am ready for the adventure, whatever state of mind I seem to be in! I try to remember everything needed, and realize I am really look-ing forward to meeting the honeybees.

I put on my bee suit, which covers me from head to toe. It is a white outfit, similar to a long-sleeved jumper, with a netted hat that zips onto the back and protects the entire body from the bees. The outfit also includes long elbow-length gloves, white socks, and white shoes. Everything I am wearing is white to keep the bees calm. They do not like dark colors and I want to keep them content for our first meeting.

Next I prepare some sugar water in a spray container and carry my first package of bees to their home in the woods. The honeybees' garden is behind our home, down a crooked path that leads to the woods. Two large thorn trees open up to a circular area that flanks the honeybees' garden entrance. As I walk through the woods to their new home it feels surreal and the feeling continues to intensify inside of me. Something in my unconscious is ignited and the space feels like I am walking in another world, where the human mind is extinguished and the heart flutters with newfound awareness. I am aware of senses, smells, and movement like glittering water twinkling around me in flight. It is as if I am seeing nature for the first time. I enter through the towering thorn trees into the bee garden and I peer inside the case of bees I am holding. There are thousands of bees moving inside the box, feverishly trying to find a way out. I spray them with a dose of sweet sugar water. This calms them down and keeps them busy licking the sugar off their bodies while I begin to work.

I gently place the first box of bees on the ground inside the circle of trees in the bee garden and ready myself. The two dif-ferent hives have already been set up and awaiting the colonies arrival. The sound of the honeybees has intensified as we journey into the woods and they are becoming very loud. I spray the entire box of bees with sugar water to calm them down a bit and I am ready to begin. Each box of bees has a circular lid attached by nails, so I gently pry the lid open. As I open the lid and peer inside I see thousands of honeybees frantically trying to get out!

I take a deep breath and slowly dip my hand into the box with the thousands of bees chaotically flying around as I try to pull out the queen's cage. I dangle my hand around and around. The queen is not there! The queen's cage is nowhere in sight and the bees are quickly coming to the top of the box in search of freedom.

My heart is beating faster than normal as I hear Bob's instruction echoing in my mind "not to take too much time." All of this is ironic since I can't find the queen, nor do I really know what I am doing. My head is still abuzz and I take another deep breath. I peer down into the cage of bees and see bees huddling around one of the corners. The mass of bees inside the box will quickly converge on the queen's cage so I need to find the queen and retrieve her. It is hard to distinguish her cage from the huddled masses swarming in fast-paced chaos within the box. I dip my hand inside the box of bees again and immediately they swarm my arm. Within seconds my hand and arm are covered with bees climbing up to the opening of the box as I gently feel around for the queen's cage.

It's a queer feeling to touch all these bees as I move my hand through the interior of the box. There are clumps of bees everywhere. They are on the floor of the box, flying around, climbing up the sides of the box and up my arm. The honeybees clump together as they climb up the sides of the box and attach to the group of bees climbing up my arm. They look like molasses being pulled in all directions while each bee moves and buzzes constantly. I must feel softly as my hand delicately touches the thousands of bees as I try to find the queen's cage. All the while the honeybees hang onto one another without a beginning or end in sight, as they drip onto one another like glue.

There is a swarm of honeybees covering something in the corner, so I figure the queen must be in there somewhere. With seven to ten thousand bees flying in this small little box, my vision is distorted as I angle my hand into the swarm of bees. Carefully I brush off the bees to finally see a corner of her cage. Slowly, I pull her cage up and brush more bees off as they hang on to me like syrup. Hundreds of bees are dangling onto each other, forming a huge dripping mass. Now the noise from the honeybees is loud and constant as it permeates everything, and an explosion of buzzing comes from the bees!

Finally, I brush most of the bees from the queen's cage, as well as from my hand and arm, and I carefully pull her cage out of the box. I use a very soft bee brush that feels like feathers to brush the honeybees back into the box and cover the entrance to keep them inside. Now I sigh gently, I take a breath and take in this moment. My hand was in a box of over seven thousand bees and it was awesome. It's a feeling I have never experienced before. I feel scared, excited, anxious, tentative, entranced, and in awe all at the same time. I quickly place a stone over the box of bees to keep them in their cage, and I am ready to prepare the queen for her new hive.

The queen's cage is a small, netted box with a hole in the bottom. The hole is filled up with candy. The candy is for the queen and her attendants, who are also inside the cage, caring for her and keeping her contained. I find it interesting that in the life of bees the queen must be taken care of by others in order to survive. Instead of asking or needing for care, it is a way of life and a necessity, just like breathing.

To prepare the queen for her new home I pierce a small opening through the candy that is holding the queen inside her box. The opening allows the attendants to help the queen achieve her freedom. By piercing a hole the in the candy covering the opening for the queen it is easier for the bees inside and outside the queens cage to eat her to freedom. As the candy is eaten the entrance widens and allows the queen to fly from her small cage into the hive with the thousands of other bees.

The queen's box is laid within the hive box and then I release the rest of the bees around the queen. Immediately, the seven to ten thousand bees fly around the queen's box, eating at the candy and trying to free her. I close the lid and sit back listening to the honeybees inside the hive. It will take the bees around forty-eight hours to eat through the candy and free their Queen. During this time the Queens scent intoxicates the entire colony and by the time the queen is free they are her devotees.

I peer through the window in the top-bar hive, watching the bees, and release a huge sigh of relief. The job is accomplished for now. The bees commune in their new hive. They are already going to work, knowing exactly what their purpose in life is, and I find myself exhilarated.

I enjoy the hum of the bees inside their hive. The sound is strong, sweet, female and intoxicating. It touches me deep inside, as if the colony of bees is singing to a deep chamber within my heart and soul.

The honeybees fly around me as I release them into the hive and I find myself enjoying the feeling of having bees everywhere around me. After releasing the honeybees into their new homes the colony first works to free the queen. Then the queen and her attendants are the only bees that will remain in the hive. The other bees will begin their work to chart their territory, creating the combs and retrieving pollen. I actually love the bees flying around me. It is as if we are all communicating together. While the honeybees fly around, a powerful lullabying quickly envelops me.

I feel relief as I leave the honeybee garden and head up to the house to retrieve the second box. My hesitancy and trepidation has receded a little as I pick the second box of bees up. Their sound carries a unique sense of power and intensity. It is amazing that such a small creature can evoke such great awe.

The second box of bees is much easier to work with, since the queen is hanging exactly where she's supposed to be. I retrieve the second queen's cage, pierce her candy to aid in her freedom, and then hang her box in the hive. As I take the queen away from the box of bees, I am aware that their sound and desire increases. They have such craving for their queen! I hang the second queen's cage in the traditional hive box and I release the remaining bees around their queen and the hum changes, it becomes calmer. Yet the hive will remain heightened and intensified until the release of their queen.

The queen and her attendants, inside their box with the candy, stay hanging in the hive for twenty-four to forty-eight hours, or until the colony of bees reach her by eating through the candy and freeing her. During that first one or two days, the queen's pheromone (or her personal scent) is released to the colony and in this short period of time the colony of bees and the queen become one.

The queen's pheromone scent is also known as "the queen's substance." As the scent of her pheromone permeates the hive box, the other bees begin to calm down. They have finally been united with their queen, and they start their work for the colony. The survival of the honeybee and its colony is totally dependent on the queen bee, and the queen bee is totally dependent on her colony; neither can exist without the other.

I sit back, looking at the two hives, and take a long deep breath, knowing that this is a good initiation with the ancient honeybee!

Four

Getting to Know You

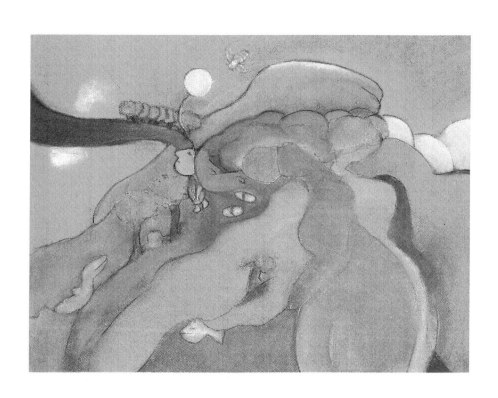

JUNE

Like the bees, we should make our industry
Our amusement

Oliver Goldsmith
1730–1774

    The two new colonies have been set up in their hives, fed sweet sugar water, and left to their own devices. After two days I am ready to check on the queens, to see if they have been released from their cages. In the top-bar hive the queen is still in her cage with her attendants. I carefully pry the small cage open and release her into the hive, among the colony of bees that have been waiting for her. The forty-eight hours gives the hive enough time to become familiar with the queen's scent and become intoxicated by her pheromone; it is now safe to release her among the thousands of bees.

The other bees fly toward her in great devotion, for she is the queen and the life giver to the hive. Soon a beautiful excited hum ensues. Then the sound inside the hive quickly changes; the bees calm down and their buzzing becomes a sweet contentment. This is the moment the honeybees have been waiting for since their initial departure.

The traditional hive box has the queen's cage dangling inside with most of her candy eaten as well. She is just about ready to be released. I assist her out of her cage and off she goes, with hundreds of bees attending to her. Her pheromone connects the hive as one, perhaps it is the glue that keeps them together, as they interlock and hang onto one another. At times it is hard to see where one ends and the next begins, because of this connectivity that they exhibit. Now that the queen is free, she will be followed and accompanied by many other bees at all times—the queen will never be left alone.

The honeybees are now alive and present in me as I work with them and the two different hives. I have come to the realization that I finally have my teacher from the natural world the honeybee, and she is ancient. This new teacher requires me to have it together when I visit, since the honeybee is very sensitive to the subtle energies around it. Anything out of balance alerts the bee and attracts the entire colony to check things out. The sweetness of a bee is equaled by the painfulness of its sting. I am learning to walk gently with this creature.

This ancient creature is very important to our world and she has an insistent voice that needs to be heard. I listen for the queen's message, and it feels much like a persistent child or constant knocking on a door. The queen bees and their colonies are now living companions on our land and in my heart. I ponder the beauty and divine alignment of our union and time together.

This message of the goddess beckons to me, as I am also in my own queen stage. The different stages of womanhood, as described in Donna Henes's book *The Queen of Myself,* are: Maiden, Mother, Queen and then Crone. I am in my queening.

I am having fun connecting the queen of myself with the queen bees on the land. The queen bee is the goddess who is one with her world, one in power, union and vision, while walking in the totality of herself. This is the perfect teacher for me.

The mythology about the ancient bee dates back as far as human drawings on rock walls in the Stone Age and across the entire globe. There are many myths about honeybees that refer to the golden nectar, communication with the gods, life-giving properties, and protection, to name just a few. In all cases the honeybee is considered to be the queen connected to the divine.

Many myths tie the honeybee to the gods and goddesses of ancient Greek mythology. The Greek tale of Zeus as a baby is also a poignant tale of the bees. Zeus is a god of Greek mythology and the son of light. Yet when he was born, his father Kronos, who was the King of Gods, wanted to kill his son Zeus. Rhea, Zeus's mother, hid him in a cave on Mount Ida, which is on the island of Crete. She did this with the assistance of the bees. According to the myth, Melissa, the powerful bee goddess, kept Zeus alive within the cave feeding Zeus sweet golden honey and mead to drink while her bee soldiers kept any intruders at bay. In this way, the honeybee Melissa and her colony of bees protected Zeus from death at the hands of his father and nurtured him with the sweet nectar of the Gods.

Melissa is the Greek word for bees and she is also a Greek goddess. Delphi is home to many goddess temples honoring the historical descendents of the bee goddess. The bee goddesses in Delphi are Demeter, Rhea, and Cyble who are all called Melissae. Rhea is the mother of Zeus and defended her son with the help of bee wizardry.

Another Greek myth regarding the bees is that of Demeter. Demeter is the fertility goddess connected with the honeyed bee who brought life to crops and plants on earth. Demeter's mother was Rhea who was the daughter of Gaia and Goddess of Earth. The God of the Underworld, Hades, fell in love with Persephone. Hades made a pact with Persephone's father, Zeus, that Persephone would live in the underworld. Once Persephone's mother, Demeter, found out about this pact she made the lands barren. Persephone was returned to earth, but in exchange for her freedom she had to return to Hades and the underworld for one-third of each year. This time in the underworld with Hades is when earth experiences winter and lays barren. In the springtime Persephone returns to earth from the underworld and there is a rebirth. The honeybee comes forth from the cold to pollinate our world.

The mythology of the honeybee regarding death, rebirth, and resurrection is associated with the Eleusinian mysteries of Greece as well. Julie Sanchez-Parodi, in her article *The Eleusinian Mysteries and the Bee*, states that, "for almost two thousand years, the Eleusinian mysteries were the most famous and influential religious cults in the Ancient Greek world. It is no exaggeration to say that the Mysteries influenced and inspired many of the greatest minds of Greece, including Aristophanes, Aristotle, Herodotus, Homer, Plato, Plutarch, and Sophocles – all of whom were initiates." The initiates through the ages and even up to present day have kept the Eleusinian mysteries secret. They hold a traditional procession regarding death, purification and rebirth each year honoring the ascent of Persephone from the underworld to experience an enlightened rebirth on Earth.

The initiates that complete the Eleusinian mysteries go through a ritual or right of passage. During these rituals the honeybee and the wisdom associated with the bee are an intricate part of the ceremony. The ceremonies were thought to give mystical rewards to the initiates themselves, who were called "mystai."

Picture of Statue of Artemis of Ephesus in Turkey

Wikimedia Commons, Vatican Museum, Rome Italy

Another goddess of Greek mythology is Artemis, a goddess connected with nature. In the statue named Artemis of Ephesia she is depicted with nature emerging from her body in the form of bees and bee eggs emanating from her breast and front. The statue of Artemis is one of two that stand in the Temple of Artemis at Ephesus, which is in Turkey. This temple is one of the seven wonders of the ancient world. During their time of power the priests were known as "Essenes" or "King Bees," and were associated with the Dead Sea Scrolls. The mythology of the Goddess Artemis holds the power of nature, magic, and shape shifting.

The Beekeeper's Bible is filled with facts and wisdom regarding bees. In addition there is a discussion of myths related to bees "Vishnu, Krishna, and Indra together are called Madhava or Nectar-born Ones, Vishnu is shown as a blue bee on a lotus flower, which is considered a symbol of life and resurrection." The mythology of the delicious sacred nectar of the bee is associated with the sacredness of the honeybee itself.

In Egypt, bees were believed to be the tears of Ra and associated with the sun. The Kung Bushmen in the Kalahari believed bees carried supernatural powers. Many cultures believed that the bee was a carrier of magic and a communicator with the divine, and honored the bee with ceremony, ritual, and festivities. In the Mayan culture, the bees were considered communicators and couriers of nourishment between humans and the sun.

The mythologies of the honeybee always refer to the golden nectar, or the nectar of the Gods, along with the divine healing properties of honey, mead, and royal jelly.

The divine food called royal jelly is the food of the queen bee. From the earliest mention of bees, there has been an association with royalty and ancient wisdom. The mythologies spoke of the gods and goddesses consuming nectar and ambrosia. The nectar for the gods is the liquid honey, and ambrosia is the delicious honeyed wine called mead. Bees and honey also appear in the ancient Indian Hindu text the Rig Veda, which was compiled around 1500–1000 BC. The Bible also refers to Deborah, the Queen of Bees, who gains an unlikely victory for the Israelites.

The myth and lore of the bee range from ancient mythologies and texts to folklore through the ages. There is much we don't know about the honeybee and there is a lot of mystery that still exists with the bee. The bee is even found upon the lands as a unique crop circle. This crop circle of a bee was recently taken on June 25, 2004 at Milk Hill, Wiltshire by Lucy Pringle. Much of the mythology about the bee is about feminine magic and creation, and below is a wonderful representation of the bee.

Picture of Crop Circle of Bee

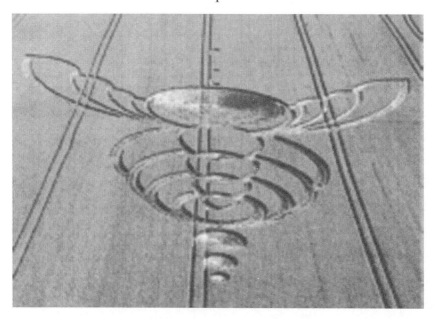

Photography by Lucy Pringle

This little bee is considered sacred in so many ancient texts, and sacred is also a way to describe the mating ritual of the honeybee. In the nature of bees the queen bee is the only female that can mate and she mates only one time in her entire life. I call it her "Magic Maiden Flight," in which she flies from the hive during her maidenhood, when she is about sixteen days old, to mate with the drone (or male) in the springtime. The young queen mates in midflight. She and the drone join together and create a perfect union for conception in mid air.

The queen can mate during this Magic Maiden Flight with more than one drone, and has been known to mate with up to forty drones. After this day-of-love feast she will never mate again during her three to five year lifespan. She has filled herself up and will lay eggs for the rest of her life from this one magical day of love.

Mating is interesting in the cycle of bees because the queen is the only female bee that mates, and she only mates during one day of her entire life; all the female workers are sterile and will never mate. They devote their lives entirely to the colony and its survival.

The mating ritual for the males is even trickier than for the females. The male drone is needed for fertilizing the queen and that is his main function in life. Once they mate, they die. The drone leaves a part of himself inside the queen and falls to his demise after this midair moment of love.

Mating then is the main job of the drones or boys and the girls do everything else. The female bees take care of the queen, as her royal attendants, nurse bees, guard bees, and the worker bees foraging for the pollen and nectar. They create the combs from wax excrement on their bodies and they create the honey, which fills the combs.

In the hive the genetics are entirely derived from the mother, since the drones don't have fathers. This means that the entire social organization of the honeybee colony is totally dependent on the female and totally run through female genetics. The queen produces male or female offspring. Though the queen needs the drone for mating the genetics are from the female and the drone is created from the queen. Drones not lost in the mating ritual lounge on the honeycombs created by the girls. If they are too lazy, and not needed, the girls guarding the hive expel the males from the hive.

There are usually about 3oo to 3ooo drones around the hive during the summer months, which is a sign of a healthy hive. The female bees will keep the males on standby for mating with a virgin queen until they are no longer needed. By fall, if there are any males around, the female guard bees may eject the drones to prepare for winter, when the queen and her colony of girls run the hive. This is an interesting juxtaposition to the role the male plays in human society.

The mating for the queen and the drone is a magical ritual of the bees. Yet, man has tried to play a hand at copying the natural world for production, enhancement, and other reasons, and making love in midair is not a part of the scientific enhancement. In 1945 a writer by the name of E.B. White wrote a song that was published in the New Yorker magazine in which he addressed the breeding of the bee through artificial insemination. He pointed out the handicap in the premise of changing the natural order of the bee, stating "what boots it to improve a bee, if it means an end to ecstasy?" A short excerpt from the poem follows:

A moment of:

E.B. White's Song of the Queen Bee

...

I am a bee and I simply love it,
I am a bee and I'm darn glad of it,
I am a bee, I know about love:
You go upstairs, you go above,
You do not pause to dine or sup,
The sky won't wait—it's a long trip up;
You rise, you soar, you take the blue,
It's you and me, kid, me and you,
It's everything, it's the nearest drone,
It's never a thing that you find alone.
I'm a bee,
I'm free.

....

For I am a queen and I am a bee,
I'm devil-may-care and I'm fancy-free,
Love-in-air is the thing for me,
Oh, it's simply rare
In the beautiful air,
And I wish to state
That I'll always mate
With whatever drone I encounter.

This poem speaks eloquently about the struggles our natural kingdom has endured along with the fun a honeybee has making love. The natural order of the bee cannot be enhanced through the hands of humans, yet now the little honeybee and the scientist are interlocked for their mutual survival; they need each other.

The magic and mythology evoked by the bee is a creative source of wonder. As I visit the hives every few days, this feeling of awe continues to crystallize within me, and I find the honeybees are a great joy and comfort. My excitement grows at the flurry of noise coming from the thousands of honeybees inside their hives. I get a lilt going into their secret garden and feeling their presence all around me. I am lulled by the bees and find myself staying longer and longer. I can spend hours with the honeybees and it feels like a small moment in time.

The pathway to the honeybees' garden is long and winding as it leads into the woods and out of sight. When I walk by the tall old trees lining the path, and through the entrance of the thorn trees, I feel as if I have entered a different worldly realm. Perhaps this is what I have envisioned as the idea of Avalon or a fairy kingdom, but this is neither of those. This is a powerful bee realm full of magic and purpose.

It feels like a haze has been cast over the area as I enter the bee's garden and it shines or glimmers. A golden light emanates from the center. The sound of the honeybees is audible once I enter the garden and blends with the sight of bees rising up everywhere I look. The garden evokes a sense of respect. Its energy is strong, feminine, creative, and has divine purpose. The play in a bee garden is quite different than a place of giddy laughter; it is a place in which one needs to walk lightly and carefully.

Daniel mowed a circular area for the garden at the edge of the woods. The hives rest on the southeast corner of the circle and the southeast corner of our land. In the bee garden the girls wake up to the rising sun and a view of the pond, which a blue heron visits each morning. The fields all around our property and beyond are filled with wildflowers. Just beyond the pond lies a path to Kill Creek, a long winding creek deep within the woods.

The northwest to southeast is also the direction honored in Peruvian shamanism as the entrance for the divine feminine forces of the universe to come into physical manifestation on earth. In studying the Peruvian mesa traditions with Oscar Miro-Quesada, a Peruvian Shaman, I learned that this northwest to southeast path is called the lightning bolt of divine illumination. The honeybees ascend from their hives with divine illumination and are a strong feminine force. They leave their dark mystical realm and enter this world toward the southeast, where the morning sun rises to awaken the new day.

Five

Everything Is Music

JUNE

I wandered lonely as a cloud
That floats on high o'er vales and hills,
When all at once I saw a crowd,
A host, of golden daffodils;
Beside the lake, beneath the trees,
Fluttering and dancing in the breeze.

William Wordsworth
1770–1850

The Hums The Hums The Hums

The beautiful sound of the hums from the honeybees fill my senses with absolute awe when I put my ear near their hive and listen to the girls inside. When I first approach the hives it is quiet—at times I cannot hear a bee at all. Then I lay my ear to the hive and this powerful vibration and soft constant sound created by the hum ensues. It takes my breath away. The sound of so many bees buzzing together is an intoxicating lullaby.

As beautiful and sweet as is the sound of the bees, the sting is not so sweet. But the honeybee's sting goes hand in hand with being a beekeeper. I actually want to get stung. I want to connect even more deeply with this beautiful creature and to feel the effects of the sacred venom; yet I find the honeybee to be a very gentle creature. She will fly around me with no concern about me at all. Many will fly near me in a giddy dance, and of course I am not bothering them, except to bring sugar water. I am not disturbing anyone yet.

I am relaxed when I visit the girls and have slowly begun visiting the hives with less and less of my bee outfit on. I enjoy not wearing the heavy attire during the hot summer days. It is also fun to have the bees so close at hand, flying around me. I will continue to give them supplemental sugar water for a few weeks and then the hive will be established enough to stop and they will accomplish all their own needs. Looking back, I realize I had become so relaxed and giddy that I was totally unaware of what was coming.

The honeybee has survived for eons due to her defense, which is the sting. The sting from a bee can kill or heal a human. It just depends on the circumstances. Or, let's say it depends on the honeybees.

Now, when I enter the bee garden, I have a little ritual. I sing to the honeybees to alert them of my presence and let them hear my vibration, so as not to startle them. Since I began caring for honeybees and singing to them, I have learned that the honeybee can't hear a thing. Yet I continue to sing to them, feeling that they can sense the vibration. Perhaps this ritual is more for

me than the honeybees. I quickly feel myself go into a sooth-
ing trance as I move closer to the hives. Watching the colony of
bees inside the hives is like seeing a fast-paced film that shows
the entire life cycle of a flower in a moment. Both of the hives
are growing a lot and both queens are proficient, which means
everything is expanding.

The top-bar hive is interesting to watch. The colony
begins with a slat of wood covered with beeswax. That is it.
Within a few short weeks the little slat of wood begins to show
the results of the bees' hard work in producing their heart-
shaped combs. These honeycombs are beautiful. They are naturally heart-shaped, filled with honey, and it's all created totally
by the bees. These creations are as beautiful and valuable to me
as a block of gold.

It seems that the honeybees work tirelessly from early
morning to evening creating sweet nectar for the combs. Yet my
concept that the honeybees are busy at work all day is actually
incorrect. The bee is quite industrious but also tends to herself
quite proficiently.

Under close observation, researchers have found that
a bee works about three and one-half hours a day. In 1899,
Professor C. F. Hodge studied bees by marking them and watching them continuously. Dr. Hodge stated, "No single bee that
I watched ever worked more than three and one-half hours a
day...with each bee napping in their combs after they worked
throughout the day."

In 1950 Martin Lindauer, an entomologist, drew the same
conclusion. He also found that a lot of the time the bees did
nothing, or very little. Though by the way a bee moves, I would
never know they were ever still. They dart back and forth in

such a seemingly chaotic motion that the last thing they evoke is idleness.

As a woman in this day and age, taking care of myself has often been put on the back burner, so this is one lesson from the honeybee that I've taken to heart. This million-year-old species has shown me that taking care of herself is just as important as any other responsibility. For a honeybee, the balance of work, rest, and play is a way of life and is a good example for me.

This glorious honeybee does all its work during the day because the sun is imperative to its life! The sun and landmarks around the hive allow the bee to create an internal mapping or navigation system. Even on a cloudy day, the honeybee will use the sun for directional purposes. Bees become accustomed to and dependent upon this internal map of their area. It's used as an imprinted directional compass. The map allows them to find their way to a nectar patch or back home. If the hive is moved, whether it is some distance or just a few feet away, the colony of bees would need to relearn their entire territory and create a new directional imprint for mapping.

The sunset is a signal for honeybees to start their voyage home. Their guidance system will shut down once it is dark. If a bee has been attracted to a special nectar or tree and doesn't head home by nightfall, she will have to spend the night where she is and wait for the sun to help guide her home the next day. Consequently, the hive is at full capacity in the evening after the sun has set and everything is dark.

Each hive begins with the number ten, with ten combs in the traditional box hive and ten bars in the top-bar hive. In the traditional box the ten combs fill up the first box. As the hive expands, I can add on additional boxes. The first two boxes are left for the honeybees to survive on throughout the year and any additional boxes are for the beekeeper.

In the top-bar hive it is best to leave at least twenty bars of honey or the equivalent of two boxes, for the bees to survive on through the year and during the winter months. The natural top-bar hive begins with ten bars and has space to expand the colony up to thirty bars. Once this hive is full I cannot add to it, and space must be created so the bees do not swarm and leave.

After just a few weeks, more than half of the bars have been created in the top-bar hive and over half of the slats are filled in the traditional box hive. As the bees fill the honeycombs their needs for space increase and so does the size of the colonies. Once the honeybees' hive is 70 percent full, it is time to add a box on top of the existing one to allow for the bees to grow. My two queen bees are healthy and producing a lot of larvae or babies, so the hives are busy, full, and expanding rapidly.

I have named my queens Sofia for the traditional box hive and Rita for the natural top-bar hive. There are many goddess names in mythology associated with the queen bee, such as Mellissa and Beatrice so I have named the bee garden after Mellisea to honor our elders, while my girls are still queens of today. I have given a lot of thought to this idea of the old and new emerging and coming together into something co-creative.

In this collaboration with the gifts and wisdom of my elders, something magnificent for the "now" emerges from the ancient. In creating something wonderfully new, the errors of the past must not be replicated, only the teachings. If we fail to do that we only create a copy of the old. So my bees have new goddess names—Sofia and Rita are the queen bees of The Bee Garden at our home in the country.

It is inspiring to watch the colonies grow. The queen bees lay eggs, and the other bees effortlessly work together to create an every expanding home. Rita and Sofia are both very fertile and their babies are beginning to emerge from the combs, expanding both of their colonies. A queen bee can lay up to 200,000 eggs in a season and up to 1500 larvae a day, which is twice her body weight—can you imagine! Producing babies is the only thing a queen bee does and she has the longest life span of all honeybees, three to five years or longer.

The queen bee is also the only bee that is given royal jelly as her only food source. The other honeybees receive royal jelly for just three days. Some scientists believe it may be the secret to a long and healthy life, as the queen's life expectancy so greatly exceeds that of the drones and female workers. The queen lives from three to four years and the drones and female workers live four to six weeks.

The queen bee's life is also very different from the other honeybees. The queen's attendants do everything for her: they bathe her, feed her, and take care of her in any way she needs, including removing her excrement. She attempts no other feat than laying eggs for the hive and cannot take care of herself.

During this time her pheromone permeates the entire colony, as the bees constantly touch one another. After only a few days the baby eggs hatch and the nurse bees begin caring for them. The babies will be nursed until the maturation stage, which is sixteen days for a queen, twenty-one days for workers, and twenty-four days for drones. With a healthy queen a hive can continue to expand as she creates what the colony needs, either female or male.

As each of the colonies expand, I experience their worlds more intimately and enjoy the dance of the bees around me while I work. The honeybee colonies expand daily and within a few weeks heart honeycombs are created and ready to be filled. The bee colonies are requiring me to be calm and at peace, while the honeybees are at the other end of the spectrum and in a space of seemingly hyped chaos.

Though the honeybee is very chaotic the bee is also very sensitive to anything around it. Therefore, it is important to stay calm and focused *at all times*. A honeybee requires the beekeeper to walk gently in its presence. In this gentle space, the harmony with the bees is magnificent. Otherwise, chaos causes the bees to create disharmony, and with a thousand bees in disharmony they can create total confusion.

I love this calm meditative state while I am with the honeybees and the enchanted bee garden fills me with sweet delight. A sense of something secret and ancient seeps into my being. As time goes by the enchantment continues to increase, as if something is flowering deep within me. A beautiful haze covers the area and also covers me when I enter this realm of the bees so that I feel myself becoming one with them. Perhaps it is the pheromone from the queen that is intoxicating me and creating this feeling of oneness.

Before leaving for a few weeks, I need to attend to the bees. The June day is beautiful as I head to the bee's garden to prepare the hives. I sing and tell the girls of my upcoming trip and how I will miss them. Up to this point, I have not been stung and have been asking for the elixir of the sweet bee for weeks. As I begin to leave the garden a bee darts intently at me, constantly buzzing and batting at my face, and then lands on my middle finger. I am stung. I am grateful and aware that the honeybee has gifted me its life and I will receive the elixir I desire. The timing is always interesting, now I am stung before leaving for a trip.

Immediately my middle finger begins to swell up as the elixir seeps from my finger out into my hand. As I head out of town, my finger quickly swells up to five times its original size. Then, both my finger and hand itch while continuing to swell up. There is just something about the itching that is inviting. The more I itch the area the better it feels. The honeybee is now present with me on my trip and during my absence from the hives. It is also great medicine inside me. My vacation trip is greatly enhanced by the fact that my middle finger is swollen to three times its normal size. The elixir of the honeybee is a very powerful healing venom and soon my aches and pains are gone. We are traveling to a foreign country where we don't speak the language, and my finger is like a beacon, except it's a beacon in the wrong place. But I am feeling wonderful.

Then a funny thing started to happen. I am now dreaming as if looking out of a kaleidoscope-shaped hexagon. In my dreamtime the view is from the mind's eye of the bee and I can hear the bees singing a soft, yet powerfully poetic, lullaby. I'm reminded of the attachment the beekeepers in my classes had to their girls. It is much like a connection to a dear intimate love.

I begin to feel a close relationship with the bee. During my dreamtime I feel as though I am one of them. I am becoming a strong bee with a sense of power and intention, and the music of the hum takes over my body

Six

Is It Day or White

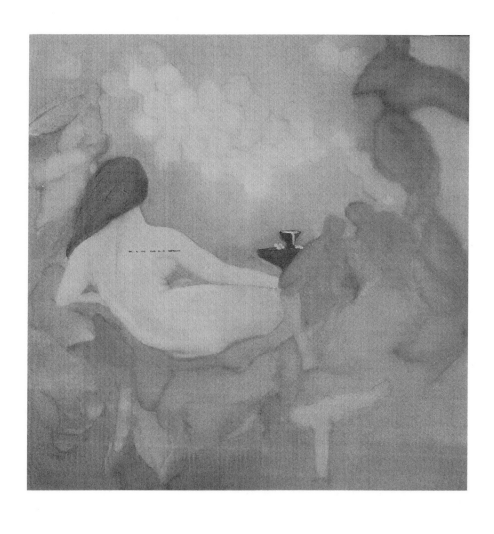

JUNE

*The least movement is of importance
To all of nature.
The entire ocean is affected
By a pebble.*

*Blaise Pascal
1623–1662*

I am excited to visit the honeybees after coming home from our trip. I prepare some sweet sugar water, lite my smoker that is filled with twine, lavender, and twigs, and go to see the bees. I am looking forward to checking their progress. I find it amazing what a bee can accomplish in a short period of time.

In just a few weeks the hives have grown so much and there are so many more bees than I remember. Honeybees do like to be left alone, and my, how they enjoyed the time alone while I was gone.

Rita and her colony in the top-bar hive are busy building heart-shaped combs. The bees are gentle in Rita's hive as I open the lid and expose the bees to the sunlight. They all lift into the air and fly around me in a whirl. Their buzzing feels much like a lullaby as they move around me in their giddy dance.

It is hot and humid, the kind of day on which you move more slowly and the heat consumes your body. Siestas become a necessity when working outside in these temperatures. Yet the bees are happy in this warmth. They fly around me in joyful play, and then off they go to forage in the bounty calling to them. The landscape is filled with a bounty of goodies and an array of colors, all calling my girls to their nectar. I close the lid and head toward Sofia's hive.

I open the lid of Sofia's hive box and find it is full. The bees are flying everywhere, chaotic and loud! This colony is feisty and more aggressive than Rita's. In this traditional box hive the bees are in total darkness, and the bottom of the two hive boxes are completely secluded and protected. For this reason, the bees in this hive are not as exposed as in the top-bar hive, and they like it that way so they are displeased with my disruption. Hundreds of bees fly out in an assault maneuver.

My sleeveless top, shorts, and tennis shoes have left my body totally exposed. Before I know it the bees attack my face and many dart at me. I am quickly stung on my face and legs. This attack from the bees is not chaotic at all. My impression is that they know exactly what they are doing. I believe they also know exactly where to attack. They prefer to be left alone and in peace, but when provoked, they are definitely not passive or afraid.

Bees will actually warn you that they are going to sting by sticking their butts up in the air and doing a little butt wiggle.

It is said that they do this three times before they begin to bat at the target and actually sting. Yet, this morning I had not picked up on any of their warnings, so it feels more like an assault and I realize too late that I am totally exposed.

My husband has been concerned about me not wearing my bee suit and the possibility of being stung on my face. And that is exactly where they headed, my face. I am concerned my face will swell up to the size of a watermelon. I apply some honey to the stings to calm the area around the spots and help with the swelling. The honey immediately soothes the itching and redness around the areas stung. My face quickly swells up and I make my first entry into the medicinal practices of honey.

There is a legend that the first Indians watched the bear as he fetched honey from beehives, and in doing so was stung many times. Once he'd retrieved the honey he lathered himself with it. Again and again the bear returned to the beehive and completed this ritual. He craved the sweet honey and ignored the stings as nothing more than a side effect of something wonderful. This legend says the Indians learned from this and followed the bear's actions. After honey was retrieved they bathed themselves with it to cure the stings and then savored the divine nectar. It is amazing what our natural world can teach us.In many indigenous cultures a union with the natural, animalistic, and spirit world is a gateway to understanding how our universe works. The communion between the human and spirit world allows the supernatural realms to come forth, bringing guidance to our human world and a greater understanding of our physicality in this ever-changing universe.

Any swelling I experience from the bee stings is minor and lasts less than forty-eight hours. I believe the affects are not as severe because I have been stung before, and have applied honey to the stings as well as consuming honey daily now.

Many beekeepers allow themselves to be stung regularly in order to attune their bodies to the venom. My own body is slowly beginning to attune to this powerful venom. This is my entry into understanding the extensive medicinal gifts of the sting and of honey. I look forward to a natural relief from arthritis and any aches and pains that are the gifts of aging.

I enjoy having a sting every once in a while and also enjoy not wearing my bee outfit. It is summer and it was hot in Gardner, Kansas, with temperatures in the upper nineties. Wearing the suit is sweltering and unbearable. There is something magical about having the bees fly all around me when I have nothing on that protects me. Though I did find there are definitely times to wear the bee suit, particularly when I need to get a lot done. Yet I must admit I have a deep desire to be stung again. I have read a lot about the healing affects of bees and I also want a deep shamanic teaching, I want to understand the honeybee in my soul.

A week after the stings, any remnants of their affects have passed. Daniel joins me on a visit to the beehives today, but we dress in opposite styles. He wears his bee outfit, hat, and gloves, while I wear a white shirt, shorts, and sandals. We head to the beehives to visit the girls.

I open the window to the top-bar hive, which reveals the entire colony without disturbing it, and then I smoke the hive to calm the honeybees. When smoking the bees the purpose is twofold. First the smoke is a calming medicine, especially when used with lavender or other aromatic flowers found in your area. Secondly, when the hive is smoked the bees get busy eating the honey for retrieval in case the hive is on fire, keeping the honey-bees busy while the beekeeper is working.

I open the top of the hive and find that close to sixteen bars of heart-shaped honeycombs have been created. This is close to double the original size. The honeybees are flying around us in a very gentle dance as I work on the hive; then I close the lid and put them to rest. Rita and her colony have grown, yet remain very calm and gentle. Though it has to be said that honeybees love their privacy and are most productive when left alone as much as possible!

I then move to the other hive and open the traditional hive box to find Sofia and her bees are suddenly everywhere. It is as if they had all got together and said, "Her head, her head." Well, that's where they headed—*my head!* Hundreds of bees, maybe thousands, begin circling around me and entering every orifice they could find. I open my eyes a little and see the bees are circling around my head as they buzz feverishly and begin to bat at my face. There are bees crawling in each of my ears and around my eyes, batting at my neck, nestling in my hair, and moving around on my arms and legs. Then they travel down my clothes. I feel hundreds of bees crawling down my back and up my shorts and I quickly become disoriented.

I think this disorientation is a defensive tactic of the bees, a spectacle of bees creating a massive state of attack that in turn creates complete confusion and disorientation. Hundreds of bees are everywhere on my body and it feels purposeful, like they had consorted together for just this moment. When bees attack they always come in herds. The girls move in clouds and my vision becomes skewed. I am aware of how off-balance I am becoming.

My head swirls in a cloudy fog of bees and I feel as if I have just stepped off a wild roller coaster into another world. I am stung over thirty times. One, two three bees are in my right ear and several in my left ear. One bee actually crawled into my right ear and nestled there before I slowly pulled it out. There are several bee stings above my right ear, a few under my left ear and many around my eyes. I also have several stings going down my neck, on my chest, and around my belly and thighs.

I quickly began to experience the venom and began to taste it in my throat, as though it were a medicinal drip in my veins. Then the humming began, or should I say buzzing; all I saw was lightness and down I went. It took me about fifteen minutes before I slowly rose to my feet and walked back to the house with my husband. I layed down on the bed and my mind became fuzzy. Soon my entire body went into a dream state.

As I slip into the dream state I am also aware of my body tingling everywhere. There are many stings inside my ears that begin to swell up. Then I hear a noise much like a door closing, but it is inside my ear. My right ear feels like a large echo chamber. All I can hear is buzzing and this palpitating breathe coming from inside my ear or my mind or from somewhere. I can hear nothing outside of me. Then the buzzing begins moving through me like a train barreling down the tracks, with a constant humming in the catacombs of my mind.

I am in a dream state within a room much like the hollows of a tree: very dark and natural with rich luxurious colors of burnt oranges, rusts, browns, reds, and golden hues that flicker and glow. I feel as though I am in an old natural setting with a rich, voluptuous plushness feeding my senses at a primordial level. I have entered the deep inner dwellings of something old and magnificent, A feeling of awe sets in.

The room is a hexagon and has windows on three walls as if open to the world, but at the same time it feels very private and hidden. It is both real and unreal and I find myself grounded in a home among the trees. Or at least that is my guess as to where I am. There are beds, or a sense of beds, everywhere in the room, giving the feeling of luxurious silk linens and deep soft cushions surrounding me.

A golden light shimmers across this room from obscure places, just as candles and crystals glow off one another and cascade around the walls. Lights come from the floor and bounce off the walls to cascade in an array of beautiful flickering lights. They are much like stars cascading across the heavens, shimmering and all aglow.

The beds are plush and inviting and, as if in a drunken spell, I am entranced by them. I feel a hand hold mine and guide me to a bed. I gaze up to see a figure but I also see nothing. Rays of ultraviolet light come from the beds, lighting up their voluptuous softness, and I am sweetly intoxicated. The huge magnificent bed seems to extend the entire length of the room, the room that vibrates and moves as if it were breathing. I fall back softly among the pillows and feel totally surrounded by someone or something evasive as smoke.

I lay comfortably on the bed and the room keeps extending out with a pulsating breath. I am not sure if there is an end to the room, yet there are windows to the outside everywhere except the back wall. The bed is located against this back wall and gives me a feeling of total privacy and absolute seclusion. The views are of woods or forests, with rich greens and different flowers everywhere. I view all this from a different vantage point than the one I know. It feels like a place high in the sky that touches the tops of the trees. It also feels as though I might be inside the belly of Mother Earth or on a totally different planet.

The room is filled with delectable goodies, candles, and jars of golden liquid. Beautiful sparkles and starlight shimmer everywhere. There is a feeling that this is "everything" in some deep sensory way. Even the smell is intoxicating and so wonderful. It fills my senses and lightness envelopes me.

My head is somewhere else, I am not sure where. I am as light as a feather and begin to float in the air, traveling on this bed of grandeur. As I lay I experience multiple realities at the same time. There are beautiful loving female bee attendants, and at the same time I am totally alone, private, and in peace. I travel to ancient cities crowded with people and at the same time lay on this beautiful bed high upon a treetop. I am dreaming and I am lucid at the same time, I am inside my body and without. It is an ecstatic realm that shifts and changes with every breath that I take.

I feel a sense of knowing that there are other living things surrounding me that are moving about with elegance and purpose. Perhaps there are invisible bees and spirits, or women taking multitudes of forms. Some of the forms are earthly, and some forms are etheric and not of this earth.

Then I become aware of an overwhelming odor. It is the scent of the divine feminine and it is intoxicating, strong, sweet, and sensual. This is such an interesting space, this space with all women. You can feel it in the air and in the energy; it is the feminine. It is the energy of a matriarchal society, and very different from the patriarchal society of my human realm. This female society is strong, powerful, and ancient.

I myself have always been attracted to men, to unions of diversity. I have contemplated the nonexistence of men in the colony of bees and how different the energy is. In their space I visit the divine feminine, the Mother Goddess, who is the bee-hive. In their space the male energy exists it just doesn't have any power.

As I experience the honeybee my life is changing to a union in which I experience a communion as well as an expan-sion, a strength and love of the divine within myself. I experi-ence the wholeness of something greater than myself invading my being. This is the emergence of something that works in union with the divine feminine scent and it is quite a magnifi-cent thing, much like the colony of bees. They work wonderfully together when their scent is connected and harmonized as one.

The queen bee visits my dreamtime regularly and ignites my imagination. I am shown colors that are so alive they drip and palpitate with a heartbeat, like the deep rich expanse of nature and they overwhelm my senses. These dreams unfold from the point of view of a multifaceted hexagon, and I become used to viewing the world of my dreams through this unusual perspec-tive. In the beginning, I was confused as to what I was seeing through this fractured view, and it took me a while to decipher what was right in front of me.

I began to think I must have been seeing through the eyes of a bee when dreaming. Then that "aha" moment hit, and I real-ized that was not what was happening. I was a bee, not just see-ing as a bee would, in this dreamland. I am a bee. I am nestled in the hive and it is warm, deep, and rich. I feel ancient and my surroundings or the permeating energy is old. It is grounded in golden hues of honey—oranges, and browns, and deep colors that give the feeling of something baroque, rich, and tasty.

The buzzing of the honeybee vibrates from somewhere deep within me, and I am never alone. I am everything and I am nothing all in the same moment. This is a rich feeling that courses through me like blood. It is a powerful sensation from the inner workings of nature that show how exquisitely interconnected the world is. This is where the elders reside in this space of heaven within nature. I dream I am in the Goddess's castle that is complete with delectable goodies and bees everywhere. The castle and its essence fill my senses and surround me with awe.

I feel one with the bees and a sweet constant communication ensues with the girls, whether I am physically with them or not. The sense of the bees and their presence is quite enjoyable. I love having them fly around and dart about my body as my reality in my waking time become intensified. My senses feel heightened and each day my step becomes a little lighter. I can still feel the effects of the last sting though the physical discomfort subsided within a couple of days and the feeling of easing muscles and a lighter step took affect immediately. I still feel as though I am breathing out of my right ear and hear the breath coming from my ear much like a heartbeat. This pulsating heartbeat and breath beat together as one in my mind.

Seven

Jelly Girls

JULY

The men of experiment are like the ant, they only collect and use.
But the bee... gathers its materials from the flowers
Of the garden and of the field, but transforms and digests it
By a power of its own

Leonardo da Vinci
1452–1519

I am finding that the importance of the beekeeper in the care of the queen bee and her colony is unlike anything I have ever experienced or known. Many times the hives want total privacy and need very little from me. Yet I provide maintenance for the hive, ensuring the queen is healthy and productive, ensuring that the hives are free of mites or other harmful carriers, and assisting in ensuring that there is sufficient water and food sources available to the bees. The honeybees' hives can multiply and produce quite a bit of honey with a healthy environment for their colonies. The size of the colony, therefore, must be maintained at all times. The queen lives anywhere from three to five years, so it is important to be vigilant and make sure the bee colony has a bountiful queen and everyone is healthy. The queen keeps the hive together for she is the colony's lifeline. Without a healthy queen, the colony will leave or die.

Honeybees are wild. There is no training a bee and yet there is a deep familiar connection that has emerged for me as if we have trained together. Though the honeybee is not a pet, the emotional connection is very similar. This relationship is much about partaking in the unique dance of nature in an intimate way, as if the goddess is holding my hand. The goddess, the honeybee, is always much more productive without interruption and the importance of time alone is being taken to heart. Caretaking involves giving the hive the time and space needed for the bees. You can actually leave them alone for weeks at a time.

Just as the beekeeper has a role for the bees, the bees are important to the beekeeper. They are imperative for pollinating our natural world, providing honey, and other powerful medicinal gifts. The bees have also enhanced my reality. I am experiencing something lying outside the restrictions of form with the relationship of the bee and the beekeeper. The rich teachings from the realm of the divine feminine are applicable to today and for myself. The queen bee is very well cared for and receives all that she needs, providing the space, the environment, and the privacy for her creations.

Just as we all see things from our individual perspective, the honeybee has opened up a new point of view for me. Not only in how I see the world and take care of myself, but also enhancing my perspective on the world. The honeybee's vision is very different from human sight. The bee sees the ultraviolet rays in the spectrum of light, which helps call forth sites for pollination. It is moving to learn from a creature that sees subtle energies that are invisible to my spectrum of vision. Humans are able to see less than ten trillionths of the entire light spectrum. In order to see the entire universe I would need to see as all species see. Then I could view the holistic reality that exists right before my eyes. In understanding the perspective of just one creature, the bee, I have been able to expand the vista within myself.

The ability to see what surrounds us is a uniquely personal perspective. As John O'Donohue wrote, "Each of us is responsible for how we see, and how we determine what we see. Seeing is not merely a physical act; the heart of vision is shaped by the state of the soul...". How we see the world determines our reality. What we see and what we can interpolate is important to our understanding of reality.

Can I explain or understand my universe if I am unable to see the entire scope of the universe, or understand the realities of other beings that coexist with me? Nothing within my being is passive as I create and construct my world. My reality and the tools I use for creation, along with what I place around me, are all-important ingredients to the creative end.

Just as a honeybee suckles from the wondrous riches on earth to create her honey and comb, so do I suckle from those wondrous riches to create and construct my world. Consequently, I want to be nourished by juicy worldly wonders, or the good stuff, not poisons and contaminations.

My sight and the constructs of my reality are important in determining how I actually see the world. "One of the most important aspects of bee sight is the ability to detect the direction of light polarization, since it allows them to determine precisely where the sun is in the sky above. Bees can see ultraviolet light, which we cannot see, but their eyes cannot receive the long wavelengths on the end of the color spectrum that we see," observed Dr. Eric Erickson. Erikson is a renowned researcher on how the bee sees the world. A bee cannot see the color red, yet a simple white flower is a colorful kaleidoscope filled with rays of shimmering blues and ultraviolet lights. The ultraviolet light within the plants guides the bees to the flowers—it actually glows to the bees and calls to them. The vision of the honeybee plays a vital role in what attracts the bee and what does not.

We have a lot to learn from the honeybee and from the natural world. What I have learned has enlarged my spectrum of information and increased my toolbox for an expansive life. With these teachings I can create something magical. As a human being I find much of my information is gleaned from the known, and there is so much to learn from the natural world that is unknown to us.

The land here in Gardner, Kansas is full of things thriving and growing. At the end of July, the temperature gets much hotter here in the Midwest, which is also known as the heartland. I live in the middle of the United States, the heartland, with bees that create heart combs—what a nice connection. For a few weeks, we have been experiencing a heat wave, with temperatures hovering around 100 degrees. The combination of heat and humidity has definitely caused me to move at a slow pace. It's a good time of year for skinny-dipping in the front pond to cool the body down and leaving the bees to their own.

The long hot days remind me of my childhood days in Texas, when we would fry eggs on the street and pop tar bubbles with our toes. Yet the honeybees are quite happy at this time of year and are able to control the temperature of their hives. The honeybees maintain a temperature of 88–95 degrees through their wing activation, which allows the colony to thrive. This wing movement acts much like an air conditioner in the summer and a heater in the winter.

After three months the colonies have had enough time to establish themselves. They are able to forage for all they need and no longer require additional supplements for their food source. This, in turn, will enrich the taste of the honey. Across the land there is an abundance of wildflowers in bloom that will affect the taste of the honey. The yellow and purple coneflowers along with the butterfly bushes around the house help attract the bees to the flower and vegetable gardens closer to the house.

Sofia, the queen bee, and her colony in the traditional hive box, have filled their bottom box along with 70 percent of their second box. I am now ready to add a third box to their hive. Once a hive reaches its third box, the beekeeper reaps the honey. The bottom two boxes of honey are left alone for the honeybees to feed themselves with over the cold winter months. There now must be over 150,000 bees in the two hives and they have started visiting the gardens around our home. As the honeybees stretch out their boundaries the land is pleasantly affected and my gardens welcome the honeybees with open arms.

A bee-attracting butterfly bush hangs over the birdbath on our back porch. It gives the honeybees a nice enticement to our home and gives us a chance to see the bees up close. Honeybees are passive when left alone, and we sit and watch hundreds of them play around the water dish just a few feet away from us.

The little honeybee can't swim and yet they love water, so the bee uses sticks and leaves as sailboats to float on the water. The bees use leafs as mats to lay on as they sip from the water below. When I water the bushes it is amazing to watch the insects rise up out of the butterfly and magnolia bushes and take flight. Suddenly hundreds of bees, butterflies, and other creatures fly harmoniously together, all without a concern about me as I stand just inches away.

I love having the bees at our back porch and appreciate the communion with them that my husband and family have had especially considering their apprehension in the beginning of this adventure. They have found the honeybees are sweet when left to their own devices.

I am receiving a deep teaching with the bees and that an inner voice has begun to emerge, a voice that needs seclusion. The feminine juices have poured into me and led me to a feeling of oneness, an unattached lightness. As a result, I find I need a quiet place away from the noise of the outside world.

Perhaps this is an echo of the beehive, the dark beautiful space filled with creative feminine energy. It also is an echo of the intense power of the honeybee insisting upon receiving that which she needs.

I've felt a sense of power awaken within myself since working with the bees. My body is flooded with a primordial source of the ancient feminine energy and I am "Being" in a new way. In this nonattachment I am connected to everything, knowing that I don't have to go anywhere to find oneness.

This desire to be alone continues to increase. I want quiet from the outside world. A space alone with nature and my beloveds begins to embody me. This is not just a desire. It is a need. I find myself selective about my time, my energies, and my space in an intimate way.

I had moved to our land to find a noise unlike that of the city, a different sound. Here in the country, nestled within the woods, the most beautiful sounds from nature are caressing me deep in my heart and soul. Among them are the voices of coyotes, birds, cows, deer, and of course the song of the bees. I listen and these voices, in harmony, feed my soul. The symphony out here in the country is the most enchanting thing I have ever experienced.

The queen bee and her colony amaze and enchant me equally. The eggs laid by the queen can become workers, drones, or other queens. The great creative power of the queen bee is demonstrated in her ability to produce either sex, albeit with the help of her colony, and through the food source given to young bees in the gestation period.

Royal jelly makes a large determination in the sex and type of bee that emerges from the hive. It is fed to all bee larvae, (or baby bees), the first three days of their lives, in which time their weight increases one thousand times. Afterward only the queen continues to receive the royal jelly as her source of food. Royal jelly is thought to be a miracle food for longevity of life and so much more.

There is a lot about bees and the colony during the gestation period that science does not yet know; but we do know that royal jelly is miraculous. It is made up of 67 percent water, 12.5 percent proteins (with essential amino acids, and hormone-like substances), 11 percent sugar, 5 percent fatty acids, 1 percent ash, antibacterial agents and a natural source of pure acetylcholine, and 3.5 percent unknown elements with traces of vitamins and enzymes. This breakdown is from *The Beekeeper's Bible*. It is used in therapeutic and medicinal remedies around the world, for both internal and external needs.

The RigVeda, an ancient Hindu Text, refers to the sacred bee and honeys with great reverence. The mythology around the foods for the gods associates the bee's honey with nectar and ambrosia. The golden nectar honey never goes bad, which is another reason it is considered a sacred food. In the Islamic tradition honey is a remedy for every illness.

The medicinal uses for honey are worldwide and stem from ancient remedies as well as new scientific research discoveries showing its many invaluable qualities. Royal jelly and other gifts of the bee are extracted from the colony and used in medicines for the treatment of asthma, viral infections, depression, fatigue, menopause, antibiotic aids, and for many dietetic concerns.

Apitherapy is the medical use of honeybee products and used by many for a variety of ailments. Bee Venom Therapy, or BVT, uses the sting of the honeybee to help alleviate symptoms such as pain, loss of coordination and muscle weakness for patients with Multiple Sclerosis. Currently, Georgetown University is studying Bee Venom Therapy with the support of the MS Association of America to determine the benefits of honey and the honeybee' by products.

Honey is also one of our first antibacterial substances and many believe that honey is still our best antibacterial aid. Many beekeepers believe in an ancient tradition that a few tablespoons of honey each day will cure all ills and ensure a long healthy life.

In association with these beliefs, royal jelly has been known to the world for decades. It is noted in a statement from the personal physician of his Holiness Pope Pius XII, Dr. Riccardo Galeazzi-Lisi. In April 1956 he stated that he attributed the Pope's recovery from a long weakening illness in large measure to his having taken royal jelly. Prince Philip of England, his daughter Princess Anne, and Princess Margaret, all have favored royal jelly. Princess Diana took it during her pregnancies. Royal jelly is found within the queen's chamber and is fed to everyone in the hive for a period of time.

The colony is also connected to one another by the queen's pheromone scent, which is also known as a complex cocktail. The queen's pheromone is secreted out of the queen's jaws as she is groomed and bathed by her attendants. The pheromone is exchanged through their bodily fluids and spread throughout the entire colony. This powerful pheromone is what keeps the colony together and allows the bees to know their hive as an interconnected entity.

Even if there are twenty different hives, all in a row, each honeybee knows her own hive by her queen's pheromone. If there is no pheromone scent for the colony of bees, or the colony is too large for the queen to patrol regularly, the hive is alerted and begins working on the colony's survival immediately. This one powerful scent, the queen's pheromone, is the hive's communication signal and life force. Without it, the colony will die. If she is unable to continue laying eggs, the hive will begin creating other queen cells by feeding the babies royal jelly. Bees can swarm (or leave) when the hive is too small or the queen is not laying eggs to continue the life of the colony. A hunter bee will go out to find a new home, and then come back and gather the group. Bees leave quickly when their colony or existence is threatened; they find a new home and move on.

If the queen is healthy and finds any other queen cells in her hive, she will immediately kill them with her stinger. This is also her way of controlling order within the hive. The queen bee is the only bee that can kill with her stinger multiple times without dying. With this system the queen and her colony have been able to exist for over 145 million years.

145 million years is an amazing time span and often comes to mind as I write about bees. I think of sweet little bees flying around during the Cretaceous Period. The meat-eating dinosaurs, including tyrannosaurs, were becoming dominant, and the plant-eating dinosaurs were declining. During this early stage of plant and flower formation, the honeybee flew among dinosaurs and early forms of birds and mammals. I picture the bees landing on the back of a dinosaur. At this time in earth's history, there were no humans in sight.

The first human is believed to have appeared between 10 and 1 million years ago. Of course, this depends on your concept of the creation of man, but this first appearance of a human was known as a hominid or a primate that walked upright. Whatever your belief system is, the honeybee has been around much longer than humanity, and she has done a good job of surviving all these centuries.

Eight

The Fields Are Alive

JULY

If you love it enough, anything will talk to you.

George Washington Carver
1864–1943

    It's the end of July and the summer is hot, hot, hot here in the heartland. The wildflowers are in bloom and the woods are covered in rich green hues with dots of vibrant color that cascade across the landscape. The land is what I call 'rolling' since in Kansas we have no large mountains or hills. The lands near us are gentle rolling slopes with lush green valleys and ponds. The wildflower plants are filled with new blossoms that flicker across the fields and through the woods.

    The bee colonies are full and busy, enjoying the bountiful array around them. This is a wonderful time for me to watch the honeybees in their full glory. Sunflowers, columbine, and paintbrush fill the fields with a rich expanse of color. Yellows, reds, and oranges fill the tall grasses and light up the fields.

In the center of the woods lies Kill Creek, a long winding creek that runs for miles across the plains much like a snake. As I walk through the fields, small animals scamper around me, darting feverishly to get out of my way. I am suddenly aware of so much bounty surrounding me: the fields, the flowers, the environment that all will affect the taste of the bees' nectar. There are many herbs, such as lavender close at hand, that will also change the taste of the honey crop. By merging together the honey with specific herbs the healing benefits of both are brought together. The fields around our home contain a bounty of medicinal goodies from our Mother Earth.

The honeybees have stretched their boundaries further across the land as each month passes by. At first the girls stayed close to their hives and in the woods. Now, there's the wonderful sight of hundreds of bees arriving at our gardens and close to the house. As I walk around our home the bees flitter from the vegetable gardens to the flowers as they sip from the different water dishes sitting out. The honeybee can travel up to five miles when foraging for nectar and my bees are spreading their little wings across the land.

I am ecstatic to see the girls everywhere I walk. Although I know they can travel up to five miles I am happily surprised to find them everywhere I go. When the honeybees come to visit our back porch they hang off a plump butterfly bush and sit around the rim of the water dish. They are fat, soft, and furry when they come for a drink and their bodies are full of pollen and nectar. They tuck the nectar into their pockets and over their bodies until they are full and can hardly fly. Once they are filled with nectar the little bees head home. To this day, it is a scientific marvel that bees can fly at all. Their wings are so thin and delicate that you can barely see them. Honeybees have four small translucent wings, with two on each side of their bodies.

As a beekeeper I notice where the bees are going for their nectar and pollen and I also notice what they like to eat. Honeybees love clover and each morning when I go to the vegetable garden there are hundreds of bees on the ground, sucking the clover. Honeybees also love berries, fruits, and lamb's ear. The bees love the goodies, whether it is a fruit, flower, or vegetable. They arrive at the beginning of ripeness, when everything looks juicy and in a state of readiness.

The flower garden is becoming more established and is filled with sunflowers, nasturtiums, morning glories, and a large array of edible treats for the honeybees. The vegetable garden consists of ten raised beds filled with tomatoes, okra, melons, asparagus, strawberries and much more, as well as a nicely stocked herb garden. Everyone is enjoying the garden, including the bees, the rabbits, the deer, the squirrels, and anyone else who comes to feast. I am trying to not add a fence and instead have lined my vegetable garden with rose bushes to deter the deer. Though the deer like the little roses for dinner as they nibble away at the roses each evening. I envision them having parties at night with all of the creatures getting together and enjoying the gifts of the garden. I definitely need to add some fencing in order to actually enjoy some veggies myself.

My knowledge of gardening is continuing to grow and I find a similar correlation between the gardens and my honeybees. Everything around the bees is important, from the source of food they are eating, to the environment and landscape they live in. For both the garden and the bees it is important to have balance, with everything working together in harmony. In the vegetable garden, growing plants that feed one another is healthy for the garden, the bees, and other creatures. For example, if you plant carrots with tomatoes the carrots love the tomatoes and they both flourish. This is called companion planting.

Companion planting consists of planting different crops together, knowing that they assist each other in nutrients, pest control, pollination, and other factors. This is a form of polyculture and allows the gardener to use a small growing space with many crops growing closely together. In companion planting, not only do the plants assist each other in productivity; they also use less space, since they are sharing. Diversity comes into play as being essential to the increase of plant production.

Diversity is also a bee's way of living as she pollinates one luscious thing to another. The bounty and variety on earth is a great gift to the honeybee; the richness of companion planting is her heavenly paradise.

This interplay within the natural world is a vital part of the whole scheme of things. I witnessed this interplay on a trip to Peru. I visited a site in the Amazon with a garden that was unlike the gardens we see here in the United States. Weeds and other plants grew together in the beds and left alone. Everything grew together and the garden flourished. In the United States we clear the land and then replant what we wish. Perhaps, instead, we should leave the land as is and integrate our growing needs in with the natural surroundings.

I am aware that I do not know the complete interrelatedness of the worlds living under my feet, nor do I know the importance of that interrelatedness to everything else. I would be foolish to demolish something I don't understand.

I have often thought that we really got it wrong somewhere in our culture on the subject of diversity. It's as if our culture is working on a backward paradigm. Instead of separating things out, it is actually the coming together of diverse elements that enables the expansion and growth of such wonders as a forest, an ocean, or a universe of stars. Nature is a great teacher and the diversity of nature is just one great example of her strength and wonder. How grand something can become when everything is part of creation and coexists; it is breathtakingly beautiful. I believe diversity furnished the seeds for the garden of paradise.

With the multitude of diverse plants that need to be pollinated I find the pollinators of the world to be magnificent and important creatures. These pollinators are essential for human survival, and, of course, for the beauty of everything emerging and blooming around us. Whether it is the gorgeous trees and flowers in our parks and gardens, the food supply, or the abundant healing gifts, the honeybee is a crucial part of our planet.

The bee carries the largest burden of our pollinators, pollinating over 70 percent of vegetables, fruits, berries, flowers, and nuts. Without the honeybee there would be no almonds, since the almond is totally dependent on the bee for pollination. Oh, how important this small creature is to our survival and that of other creatures! As John Donne wrote, "No man is an Island."

My first year as a beekeeper has been devoted to becoming acquainted with the honeybee and establishing the beehives. The honey created the first year is often left for the bees, since the production is just beginning and is usually small. With the summer season behind us, my bees have created enough honey to feed their colonies through the long cold winter months. The two bee colonies are both continuing to expand. The natural top-bar hive is a little different in that I can't expand this hive and it can't get too crowded. In the top-bar hive, as the colony expands, I will take out finished combs to create more space for the bees. In creating space for the bees I also get a beautiful treat, a heart-shaped honeycomb. The honeycombs I receive are now filled with honey and dripping on the sides. The honey is so delicious. As the thick beautiful honey drips down my fingers, it tastes like a bit of heaven. It is also very beneficial to have honey from the area I live because it is acclimated to my environment and therefore acclimated for my personal needs.

I place any of the excess honeycombs in a large glass pan with a tightly sealed lid to keep the bees out, and I receive an ample amount of honeycomb to chew each day. The honey needs to be sealed to keep it fresh and keep the bees at bay. Otherwise, they will come to share the bounty, and bees are really, really persistent. The honeybee doesn't give up!

Honey was not why I became a beekeeper. For most of my life I have not eaten much honey; it always seemed so rich to my taste buds. Now the sweet elixir of honey is quite tasty to me and I eat several tablespoons every day.

There is an old wives' tale that says if you consume a few tablespoons of honey each day you will be healthy for life. It's also been said that you can survive on honey alone since it never goes bad! So instead of stocking up on foods for backup, we could load our cabinets with honey. Perhaps honey, bread, and water are the essentials for our survival. This was also what was fed to many of our idols and gods in our mythologies across the world.

As time goes by, my dreams about the bees continue to unfold each night. The dreams always begin with the same fractured view of the hexagon. They are lovely and also odd dreams. I enjoy dreamtime in this exotic kaleidoscope and sometimes I am aware that I am dreaming. David Eagleman states in his book Incognito, "Asleep vision (dreaming) is perception that is not tied down to anything in the real world". Dreams are a state of consciousness that we do not have a fix or hold to anything and allow the un-believeable to happen.

My dreams are definitely in a place that has no fix or hold on anything, and also somewhat infinite and cozy. This dream space is constant and yet always moving at the same time. It seems I am always traveling and in a space of awe. The dream always begins with an array of colors. I am speechless as the colors come alive and drip across my mind's eye. The colors move with a palpitating breath. Caramels, golds, browns, reds, and oranges are all aglow as I view things from inside something, inside this hexagonal kaleidoscope.

My dreams begin with me lying inside the honeycomb as I experience myself as a bee. I am in a lush golden bed with cascading colors flowing around me, much like a mesh that is perfectly aligned with my body. The colors are glowing and vibrating within and around me and become one with me. The mesh feels like sacred geometry that is pulsating with every breath I take.

Then the scene changes and I am suddenly lying on a flower with the sweet nectar covering my body as I merge with the flower and feel one with her. It is as if I am moving inside and outside of the flower at the same time. I am making love with nature using all of my senses.

The flower is soft to my arms and legs and a little fuzzy, as I lie cupped in her petals and suckle her nectar. My senses are filled with the flower's intoxicating aroma and the sweet juicy nectar. My dreamtime senses evoke great wonder and beauty and awakens these within me. The dictionary defines senses as any of the special powers by which a human becomes aware of things, such as sight, sound, taste, touch, and smell. To me being sensual is to experience the subtle energy and senses that can move our heart and soul.

My soul is soothed as I play in this altered realm as a bee. I am swaying on a branch feeling the wind at my back, and my vision is filled with color. The world appears so big and beautiful here from the perspective of a little bee. I dream of flights with bees, being in swarms, and flying together as one, or find myself cradled in some succulent flower. Within this dream space my flights become a thrilling adventuring from one ethereal space to another.

Night after night, I dream of being in spaces that only exist within my imagination. I fly high over the forest and then I am nestled on a branch, or resting within a flower. I find myself in cities that are ancient as time stands still. I am soothed by the tides of the wind and warmed and guided by the sun. For many nights I find myself aroused. My heart flutters and I dream of bees as I try to determine where I am in this odd dreamscape. My vista in these dreams is always as a bee. I am always amazed at where I end up and what I see. The dream leads me to heavenly spaces, distant villages, both earthly and not of this earth. Then this white-yellow pulsating light appears and suddenly the light is all I see. It envelops my total being.

By the afternoon the birdbath fills with bees. The bird-bath looks like a sold out stadium, with all the bees lined up on the sides of the dish and many floating on their boats in the water. More and more bees learn about the birdbath by a dance called the "wiggle dance" they use to communicate. When a bee finds something wonderful, a bounty of wildflowers, a garden of delectable goodies, or a butterfly bush hanging over a birdbath, they go home and tell the colony.

First, she dances in a circle to get the colony's attention. Within this circle the bee dances by putting her butt in the air and waggling. Then she proceeds to show, on her directional circle, exactly where the colony of girls needs to go to find the treasure. All bee colonies have this waggle dance and it is a great tool for communication within the hive. Consequently, if you see one bee, more will surely follow. Whether building the sweet nectar or suckling from flower to flower, they are never alone. A bee always travels with her girlfriends or they are nearby.

I find the Sensuous Spell of the Bee, this play with the girls, heightens my senses. Spending time with the honeybees has allowed a growth in the energies within myself and I am more sensitive to the subtle energies around me than before, and in that space a desire for lightness to surround me has over-whelmingly invaded my being. I find an exquisite beauty in sur-rounding myself with those energies that soar as I drink from the sweetness that exudes from the bounty on earth.

My thoughts, words, energies, actions, and what I place around me are important in regard to what I wish to feed myself with. Perhaps they are my flowers supplying the nectar and pollen for my building blocks to my creations. These building blocks are important to nurturing myself. I enjoy the growing sweetness within and without from this little honeybee.

I am also aware of a powerful feeling growing inside me that is quite maternal; I am becoming a protectress of my bees, the land, my beloveds, and myself.

Nine

The Heartbeat of The Divine

SEPTEMBER

Choose only one Master—Nature.

Rembrandt
1606–1669

I had been having stomach problems for months and the pain was excruciating. Daniel and I started off for the hospital and I was bent over with stabbing pains. As we drove I begin to get very hot. Sweat formed at the base of my neck and this awful nauseating feeling enclosed me. I was rolling down the window when it all shifted, everything just shifted.

I stopped breathing and rested in this space in the heavens. I saw my old reality in some weird framework and then there was darkness, much like a beehive. It was totally dark and I could see nothing. Then a point of light appeared and slowly a beautiful pure radiant white space began to emerge before me.

I knew, then, that I was part of everything that exists or has ever existed and a beautiful sound slowly consumed me, it was the music of the spheres. The music in the universe was vibrating and singing intimately to me as if it was a special love song. Within every fiber of my being I was connected to everything and everything radiated a space of pure love and oneness.

I wasn't standing on anything. I was floating in space outside the form and physicality of my body and was aware that my body was not relevant to me. I was form and formless, and it felt good. I was weightless in every sense of the word. Time was irrelevant. I knew I had stopped breathing as I rested in this space of breathlessness, as if I had all the time in the world. I had no pain and I enjoyed this effortlessness, this lightness, this heightened feeling that emanated from within and without my body.

A vision of light, love, and my beloveds slowly emerged before me and enfolded me in a space of wonder. I experienced this without fear, worries or pain, only pure love. There was a place of beauty I was being urged toward as someone or something close to my heart reached out a hand to guide me closer. I quickly became aware of memories flooding in as this place emerged before me and a distant reality awakened. Somewhere within me something changed and my reality takes on a new awareness and view of the world around me. A strong feeling of homecoming quickly began to fill my heart and soul.

Then I heard my name being called by my beloved "Karrie Marie, come back to me, Karrie Marie, come back to me," and I turned to my left and saw my beloved Daniel. Daniel was standing in a golden field, with a light breeze blowing through his long brown hair and the view of the woods echoing at his back. I realized that I had to make a choice, and that time mattered. I could not be in both places at the same time anymore.

My heart was still. On my right I felt the most wonderful sensation in the universe, a long forgotten home in my heart and a place without form as I know it. This place and feeling that were shown to me felt wondrous. Then I turned to the left and another beautiful world emerged, filled with my beloved, my children, and my family, filled with the ecstasy of Mother Earth. In both worlds and realities I saw paradise. Although each holds a different space of paradise, they are both paradise. Divine ecstasy is everywhere, in the white light and also in the gaze of my beloved calling me home.

This event happened to me years ago and yet it feels like yesterday. Energy connects the entire universe, from the smallest atom to the largest star, creating this experience I am having here on earth. There is more to this earthly delight than what I know as my reality. I am on one journey here on earth while there is also a reality that exists beyond the framework I call earth.

There is not an end after death. Instead, I saw a returning to something ancient, wonderful, an all encompassing love and comfortableness. I saw and felt divine love within and without and I felt my beloveds, along with the effervescent taste of oneness cascading and permeating my being.

In this altered space communication was not with my five senses. It was with my mind, my heart and my soul. I was using senses from within my body, not without. I was hearing without being spoken to and became aware that the five senses I so depend on, here on earth, were not even accessed in this other reality. In this other space neither words nor any other physical attributes were needed to communicate with everything around me, and I mean everything. The awareness that everything is alive became absolute for me in this gifted moment of breathlessness. I also became aware that the human being who uses only the five senses could not perceive a lot of what was alive.

After this experience I find communication with nature and my flowers almost like a dialogue, a very soft angelic dialogue. The sounds from the natural world begin to pop out at me—not like noises, but like thoughts, feelings, visions, and always feelings of wonder and love. I began to see ethereal flowers dancing and talking with the physical flowers in my garden.

My senses are getting fined tuned. I realize the energetic realm that nature dwells in is that which resides in the heart, not the mind, and I suddenly see a heart dance among nature. My thought is this: Who is the intelligent entity here? The natural world resides in the absolute space of the heart and has little room for anything else.

I really love this heart space in which nature exists. It feels wonderful and emanates a feeling of completeness. It is easy in a simplistic way. There are none of the worries that we have so heavily put upon our backs. Instead, it is a sense of day-to-day pure being and oneness.

Now, years later, I find spending time with the honeybees gives me this doorway into the ultimate divine space I remember from that day I stopped breathing and saw the white light. It is a sensation that fills me with the heartbeat of the divine.

The feeling I remember of the divine is something that is harder to hold onto in this earthly realm, with its news of killings, poverty, wars, riots, fires, monetary problems, ego, etc. Our consciousness creates our reality, and what we see is our own creation, so the pure consciousness of divinity is a great source of change, a change in our perceptions and our reality.

Sitting in nature and becoming one
With the world around me
In all her natural glory
Is a very grand thing to do.

Through this first season with the honeybees I have come close to the girls and I find a great respect for the space of things I don't yet know. I watch these creatures create earthly delights wherever they are—whether in the jungles, the farms, or on mountaintops. They are located in towns and in remote areas we are not even aware of—and all these places are magical whether we see them or not.

I have thought about the savant who goes out into the world with nothing, to live as one with nature and to live alone without human contact. I have also heard the theory that more good is done when we work together, and yet I believe the individual as well as the communal are needed. I believe that one is not greater than the other. They are both important, and here again, diversity is imperative. I need all the pieces to create the puzzle.

The energy created in a space of complete union with the natural world is heavenly, and I soar in this ecstatic space. This greatness affects everything around and within me. Whether it is seen or heard is really irrelevant, especially to the natural world. The beautiful pure energetic created from nature spreads out like a ripple in the pond touching everything, carried out through the winds and tides, moving across this magnificent earth.

The saving grace and connections to these powerful wonders are our natural places for the heart of humanity: the rainforests, mountains, rivers, and oceans. The places of pristine sacredness, these quiet spaces in nature left alone by humanity are powerful places for our wellbeing as well as everything that coexists on earth. In the dance of diversity, just as the bee goes from flower to flower drinking and pollinating, I wish to dance and drink from the full range of nature's gifts. I need to honor the savant living alone as well as the loving heart that rests among the communities of humans. Only in diversity can we achieve the Garden of Eden.

Here in Kansas I am working on my Garden of Eden. Everything is thriving since the addition of the queen bees and their colonies to the land. Most flowers and plants in bloom will attract the honeybee. It is amazing to watch hundreds of bees land on a lamb's ear plant or favorite source of nectar within the trees. The bright beautiful array of colors enlivens the landscape and the honeybee delicately works from one budding thing to the next for its grand purpose: the creation of honey.

Everything a honeybee takes nourishment from will affect the taste and color of the honey. The honeybee travels for miles, foraging through large areas for pollen and nectar. Many beekeepers will plant specific gardens for the honeybees to enhance the honey's taste. For example, for lavender honey, the beekeeper will plant a bounty of lavender bushes near the beehives to ensure the honey tastes of lavender. When planting specific bee gardens the beekeeper is also keeping the honeybees close to home. They can travel great distances but will stay close to home if their needs are met.

In the beginning of summer the color of the honey is very pale, whereas if the honey is allowed to cure in the hive during summer, it turns a dark golden color. Some beekeepers wait and let the honeycombs rest in the hive until the following spring. Honey that is left over the winter months is very dark, almost like the color of rum.

We have now reached the end of summer and the bees are everywhere: in the vegetable garden, in the flowerbeds, even deep in the woods. I find comfort in their company as I work in the garden or walk through the woods. When I walk down the wooded path to the bees' garden I find myself relaxing. Slowly, the secret bee garden appears. By the time I reach the entrance to the hives I am in a meditative state. I sing to the honeybees to alert them of my arrival, and then I pass between the two large thorn trees and turn east toward the hives. Though the bees can't hear my song I am certain they feel my presence; it is my way of ringing the bell for the girls.

At noon the bees are foraging for nectar and the colony is at its smallest. It is a good time for me to work, with little disruption to everyone. I slowly lean down, placing my ear next to the hive to hear the sweet hum from the bees in the top-bar hive. At first the hum is soft, then it slowly becomes stronger and stronger as I move closer into their hive.

During the day when many of the bees are gone there is little action outside the hives except for the guard bees. But there is always a constant hum within, and it is wonderful to hear them all buzzing as they become alerted to my presence. Inside the hive are the queen bee and her attendants, the babies and their nurse bees, the creators of the comb and honey, and, always, the guard bees. The guard bees will hold watch on the outside of the entrance to the hive as well as posturing themselves inside the hive itself. I picture the guard bees in outfits much like the guards at Buckingham Palace, and all standing at attention with their little swords.

The top-bar hive is always the first hive I visit. Rita and her colony of bees have increased quite a bit, though it is hard for me to really determine how many bees are there as they fly chaotically around. I am sure there are at least five times more bees in the beehive then when I began. When I open the top of the top-bar hive the entire colony of bees is exposed. The hanging wooden bars are encased with beeswax and honey and thousands of bees rise up as the lid opens.

To create a honeycomb, six bees come together and each takes a side of the hexagon. Within the hive the six bees create one hexagon at a time on top of the comb slats. The hexagons created on top of the combs are the homes for the babies and then for the creation of the honey, which is deposited within each hexagon. Once the area is filled with honey, it is then sealed. All of this is done at a precise temperature, which is created through the flapping of the honeybees' wings. As the bees create their honeycombs naturally, without the aid of the perforated comb, the hexagons come together in a heart-shaped comb. The top of the heart is connected to the bar, and they work downward toward the bottom of the hive to the point or tip of their heart comb.

Sometimes the combs need cleaning to keep the newly created combs and honey off of the hive's lid. The beautiful heart-shaped honeycombs are attached to the hive by a thin line of beeswax that is placed on top of the wooden bar. There is a high probability that at some time a comb will fall off from the weight that they bear when full of honey.

In my top-bar hive there are two combs that have fallen. One comb had fallen a while ago, and I left it in the hive while it is full of babies. That comb is now full of honey and I am able to retrieve it, along with another comb, in order to clean the space and keep enough room for the bees to continue growing. Honeybees need space and they also like their hives to be clean at all times. The worker bees will clean up and remove any debris within the hive and remove any bees that have died as well. Consequently, the honeycomb and honey itself are always created under exact conditions, producing a very healthy and pure product.

After the top-bar hive I go on to check on Sofia's traditional box hive. There is a queen excluder that I put between the second and third boxes to ensure that the queen does not lay any babies in the upper hive boxes. The upper boxes are where I retrieve the liquid honey for myself; I want to keep the babies separate and with their queen. Yet that can also inhibit the bees from coming up to the additional boxes, especially in their first year. There are three boxes now on the traditional hive box and they have been in a dark seclusion for weeks. This hive is much larger than the top-bar hive and there must be at least ten times more bees here than in the beginning.

I open all the boxes so I can look at the comb slats that lie inside each box. I look at each slat in the hive to check on growth and honey production, as well as disease and other needs that might arise. There are nine slats in each of the upper boxes for the honeybees to create their honey on. When I smoke the honeybee's entrance I notice there are many female guards on duty. Once smoked, they go inside the hive to warn the others and then come to check me out. Luckily, I am wearing my bee outfit and their attack is dispelled. The third box is still empty so my crop will be small this first year. The bottom two boxes are filled with rich liquid gold. When I lift them up to check the lower boxes I am amazed at how heavy they are. Each box has nine large perforated combs filled with honey on each side and must weigh over sixty pounds each. The combs and hives look good. I put them all back together, close the hive up and place some rocks on the top to secure the lid against being opened by creatures.

As I gather my supplies I become aware of the circle of bees around my head. The girls have a way of communicating with each other and getting the whole gang involved. As the girls continue to circle my head and bat at me, I slowly begin walking toward the house. The circle of bees stays with me for part of the walk through the woods and up the hill. Then their sound changes from irritation to a calming buzz and the frenetic flying and batting around my head ceases. Their movements change from sharp agitation to ease and fun. The bees then retreat to their home while I continue walking to mine.

Shaded by a very old grandmother tree, I sit down on a bench in the backyard and begin to take off my beekeeper's suit. It is very hot in the suit and I am looking for relief. Sweat is rolling down my back and neck as I become saturated with moisture. Now, I know these bees are insistent about buzzing about me and yet I still take off my suit. I am hot and sweaty as I glide my glove off my left hand. One of the bees lands on my ring finger and immediately stings me. The other bees begin to fly around my head in circles. At first the buzzing is firm and aggressive. Then it becomes a dialogue or conversation as the girls fly in circle after circle around my head for over ten minutes. I become mesmerized, with a light-headed feeling, and then off they fly.

The bees take off in search of something wonderful but the sting of the one little bee stays with me. The sting is quite amazing and very therapeutic. It's on the joint of my ring finger, so the ring is the first thing off. My finger quickly begins to swell, tripling its original size. I remove the stinger and in its place is a red sore spot. The actual sting is very quick and I find that on my back, arm, neck and legs the sting doesn't bother me after a very short moment. When I am stung on my fingers and my face, however, I swell up like a balloon and the skin stretches to accommodate the huge mass that has suddenly appeared. I taste the venom at the back of my throat. The area around the spot that is stung becomes very red, then sore, then it expands, and finally the itching begins.

The medicinal venom quickly begins floating through my hand. This tingling, itchy sensation extends to a three-inch radius around the spot that was stung. Although the initial prick of a sting is quick, the stinger is often left in the wound and continues to release venom for up to fifteen minutes or until it is pulled out. I gently rub my hand and the venom slowly seeps into areas around the initial sting. The massage actually feels good and is calming to the affected area.

The best cure I have found for the irritation, redness, and soreness from a sting is honey or any honey by-product. However, I haven't found the best way to apply pure honey without dealing with the stickiness. I have also found applying royal jelly to the area works great. The swelling stays for about 48–72 hours. Then the swelling goes down and the itching starts a very intense somewhat lovely, itching.

When I scratch the area of the sting the sensation feels so good. It is almost weird how good it feels. I have found it is like an ecstatic moment — oh my, it feels so wonderful. I am like a dog moaning with ecstasy as I itch that perfect place and the rest of my body stands still. The swelling will last a couple of days, and then all goes back to normal.

The honeybee usually warns me quite loudly and persistently when it is about to sting, though when I have hundreds of bees around me it is a little harder to notice their warnings. I now consider the stings to be a sweet gift from the honeybee that creates a deep soul connection between the two of us. The sensation of being woven into the fabric of nature is huge. Now when I look across the lands I don't see "the land" anymore, or at least not in the same way. Instead, with this primordial connection to nature, I see myself when I view the lands, and the vista is personal.

Every time I leave the hives to head up the wooded path for home I have several companion bees that travel the path with me. It feels like guard bees are escorting me home, as if they are keeping me safe on our walk.

Sometimes I stop at the entrance to their garden to hear their song. It is like a conversation; they hum and sing, I listen and silently respond. Many times they follow me to the bench and buzz around my head until I stop to listen. It is like a ritual. I stop and sit, and find myself always moving deeply into a meditative space.

When communing with a honeybee it is best to stay calm and gentle in my movement. In that space the honeybee seems to calm down, or at least her attention shifts to a space of tolerance with me. The companion bee stays with me for this ritual and buzzes around my head in circles for ten to fifteen minutes. There is an insistence in the bee's energy and the constant rotation around my head makes my equilibrium teeter.

In this space I feel dazed but also alert and present, while the bee continues to buzz chaotically around my head and face, circling and circling and circling. Then the idea of time becomes unreal. Time often seems to stand still for me while I work or meditate with the honeybees. If I am in a hurry or don't sit down, the companion bee will start to bat at my face and will only stop when I stop, listen, and still myself. Nature can be a gentle and an insistent teacher.

At first I am startled to have a bee following me home, spinning around my head and batting at me. I am aware that she does not want to sting me, yet she is persistent in this dance around my head. The honeybee really seems to like going after the *head*. I feel like a child being scolded by my teacher until I sit down and converse with her. During this moment I feel her presence intimately before she flits away. This is not the queen and I am sure a different bee takes the role each time as the companion bee. Yet the pattern is the same. The bee calms down once I have stilled myself. Her insistent circling around my head stops as she sits on my neck or hand and sits still. The honeybee is teaching me to quiet my mind in order to visit the divine.

In this stillness the bee's song changes to a calm melody. Instead of batting at me for attention, she starts to dance around me in a sweet lullaby. I am taken to a pristine space right in the here and now as I see the magnificence of this beautiful creature. At times we visit for a long time. This intimate communion I feel between myself and the honeybee is powerful and moves something deep inside me. The honeybee dances and communicates with me during this moment of oneness, and I sit and listen to the language of the bee.

Resistance is not the way to win over a bee, or anything else in life for that matter. While learning to talk intimately with the bees, I find my impulse to resist fading away. Opposition is the normal reaction when a bee or insect comes to visit or attack. We instinctually swat it, kill it, or fear it. With honeybees the reaction must be calm or the bees become even more aggressive, almost as if they feed off fear. All my fears, confusion, haste, all the things that stop me from being fully present are not the way of the bee. I've come to see these distractions as illusions created by my mind. Now I enjoy the peaceful feeling that the honeybee insists upon.

The connection developing between the honeybee and me is brought about through time, communion, trust, love, and, of course, the sting, which also connects me at a deeper level to the queen and her colony. I feel a deep love or connection with the bees, much like the deep connection I imagine the bees have with each other. As time passes I enjoy this sense of passion for a different art form: the honeybee. She is a creative, imaginative exquisite creature.

Ten

A New Day

SEPTEMBER

"Now I am going to reveal to you something which is very pure, a totally white thought.
It is always in my heart; it blooms at each of my steps...
The Dance is love, it is only love, it alone, and that is enough...
I, then, it is amorously that I dance:
to poems, to music but now I would like to no longer dance to anything but the rhythm of my soul"

Isadora Duncan

September knocks on summer's door with cooling weather and long nights. The dance of the honeybee across the fields that shimmer with heat is a grand sight, but soon they will move inside for the winter. Autumn is a beautiful time in Kansas and brings lower temperatures and night breezes after a long hot summer. The trees begin to change color and more animals appear on the land. This is a time of transition for nature as everything prepares for the cold of winter. The honeybee colonies also prepare for change. Their production begins to gear down and the dance within the hive shifts with the season.

I am suited up in my white beekeeping outfit and ready to work on the hives. I have filled my smoker and brought along a bottle of sugar water. I may be in the hives for a while and want to keep the bees as calm as possible. The weather is beautiful, with temperatures hovering around the 80s. It's noon and the sun is shining overhead as I walk down the path to visit the girls.

First I smoke Rita and her colony in the top-bar hive and peer into the window. The heart-shaped combs are full of honey and have a wild appearance compared to the honeycombs in the traditional hive box. Rita and her honeybees are quite happy. They flit around their hive and the thick golden honey drips from the combs. For this hive I am condensing the bees' space and taking care of their winter needs so they will stay content and warm through the cold. Then I head for Sofia's hive. The traditional hive box is completely full of honey and will ensure a good supply of food for Sofia and her colony during this time of year when production of honey slows down.

When fall is approaching, the hives are treated for varroa mites and other harmful bugs. The bees' space is also condensed to help reduce their workload. The smaller hive allows the bees to heat and control the temperature of their environment, as well as providing a supply of honey for the beekeeper.

Every beehive has an opening at the bottom that allows the bees to travel in and out during the winter. The hive entrance is also closed up a bit to stop both intruders and the bitter cold from entering yet also leaving a space for the bees.

In the traditional hive, any additional hive boxes above the first two are removed for the extraction of honey, then cleaned and put in storage. This is also the time of year when the hives are checked for any other needs the honeybees might have.

There are many ways to accomplish the same task and beekeepers each have their own differing opinions and ideas in the matter. Whether we are talking about taking care of mites or the collection of honey, there are choices to pick from. Many beekeepers leave the opening of their hive alone so that the hive entrance doesn't get clogged with dead bees and the colony can always get in and out.

As time goes by, the life of the worker bee is completed and it dies, falling to the bottom of the hive. The colony of bees will continue to keep their home clean by removing anything that doesn't belong in the hive, including the deceased bees. Therefore, adequate space is needed for moving in and out of the hive at all times of the year. The bee colony is a clean place and when anything appears in the hive that is not supposed to be there or no longer thrives, the bees remove it.

The honeybees will also hold their excrement as long as needed. In cold months, they wait for a nice day to leave the hive and to release themselves. The honeybee can hold her excrement within her body for long periods of time and she does not release herself within the hive itself, if possible. Therefore, it is important to keep the hive doorway open at all times of the year. I am sure the honeybee must feel like bursting as she waits for a nice day to release herself in the cold winter months. I envision hundreds of bees running to the door for relief.

Once the hive has been winterized, by caring for the mites or other unhealthy bugs, the space is condensed as much as possible and the honeybees are left alone. I am finding being a beekeeper is a lesson in time and patience as well as a lesson in letting go. After the hive is prepared for winter I will not see the honeybees until next spring, The queen will continue to lay eggs to maintain the colony, yet honey production stops or slows down considerably. As the days get colder the honeybee stays inside the hive and only leaves when it's warm outside. Through working with the beehives I am aware that the colony of bees and the queen are in charge here. Make no mistake.

There is no hibernation in a beehive over the winter. Yet, the colony is in a different mode, a slow mode to some degree. The honeybees will stay in a close cluster within the hive, maintaining the colonies survival. Their ability to control the hive temperature by the movement of their wings, both during warm hot months and cold winter days is remarkable. The temperature is very important and is kept exact for making love, laying their larvae, nursing the bees, creating the combs, and creating honey. During the winter months each honeybee also takes care of itself by storing honey in its body as food to be ingested.

Over the winter honeybees form a winter cluster within the center of the hive to keep their queen and the entire colony warm. This cluster is formed in the middle and warmest part of the hive, whether in a top-bar or a traditional hive. The cluster of bees forms a doughnut shape with the queen and the nursing bees in the center. The worker bees keep the queen and the nursing bees at a temperature of 93 degrees, and the bees just outside the cluster within the hive maintain a temperature above 45 degrees. All of this occurs within the center of the hive and the honeybees stay in this shape for the winter. Within this round cluster inside the hive the bees can activate their muscles to flap their wings and control the warmth of their home.

As the bees in the inner sanctum become warm, they move out in a cylindrical fashion, so that all the bees are continually warmed as they move in and out of the core. In this fashion they all share the warmth. This cluster of bees expands and contracts, depending on the temperature outside and inside of the hive. In a sense, the cluster breathes with the needs of the colony.

The girls will continue to forage on nice warm days but their active time will wind down. Late summer in the country is still full of wildflowers: marigolds, roses, butterfly bushes, and several types of plants around the ponds. I next move to the traditional box, with my queen Sofia, and smoke around the bees to alert them of my arrival. The girls are astir and the air fills with hundreds of bees—no, thousands of bees. Their sound quickly intoxicates me. I dust the honeybees with powdered sugar to dispel any remaining mites from their bodies and my hands become coated with bees. They connect to one another and dangle off my hands and arms, dripping like molasses. It is as if they have all come out of their hives in droves to taste the sugar while I pull out the last comb to check it. The sound of the bees become louder and louder and louder.

I brush the girls off of me so I can see to work with the hives. Bees are everywhere, dancing around the hives and dancing around me, attracted to the sweet powdered sugar that is all over the area now.

There are more bees flying around than I have ever experienced. My reaction is twofold: frightened and elated. Perhaps the bees are angry, excited, and ready to attack me. Perhaps they are flying around me in elation. They are on my body, within my bee suit and even within my clothing. Any bees that have climbed inside my bee suit will be trapped and sting me as I finish preparing the hives for winter. The honeybees exit the hive in droves and are everywhere now.

I begin to feel light and I am taken back to a childhood memory of my neighborhood beekeeper. I remember this moment during which he worked with his bees and they all flew around him in a flurry. To the casual observer it would look frenetic and as if they were ready to attack, yet they were not attacking. They were having fun dancing and communicating.

Now, in my own bee garden, it's a moment the flurrying bees and I share as one, and all my resistance falls away. I feel the remembered awe of my childhood as I watched the beekeeper with his bees, but this time I am the beekeeper dancing with a thousand honeybees.

I have a container filled with some heart-shaped combs from the top-bar hive and I leave twenty combs in the hive for the honeybees. As I round up my gear and walk through the woods the bees still dance around. This time, hundreds of bees follow. I walk up the path to the house and the bees come along, flying and buzzing around me with such intensity. Perhaps it's because the end of the season for the honeybees is approaching and they are making their own preparations for the long winter nights. I go to the backbench, sit down for a rest, and watch the bees come toward me. It is like watching a cartoon of a large whirl of bees. I begin to wonder if I have honey or sugar on my suit as a trail of bees head straight my way. They are circling me as I slowly sit down.

My head fills with their humming. There is a primordial feel to the sound of their buzzing and constant movement. I am instantly in an altered state, unable to move or look at anything. The bees constantly dart about my face and body. The sound of a thousand bees so close to my senses intensifies and noise becomes overpowering. I calmly take a few deep breaths and go into a heart meditation, a meditation that centers me and changes my focus by moving the brain in my mind to the brain in my heart. It is a beautiful meditation created by Drunvalo Melchizedek that brings the human heart into the same heart space as the natural world, the space in which the whole animal kingdom resides.

I meditate into my heart and the buzzing shifts from a chaotic circling around my head and body to a convergence of bees at the back of my head, right at the nape of my neck. After a few minutes the circling ceases and they form a ball behind my head. Then the buzzing becomes different, perhaps because they are all together. The buzzing becomes one, as if there was only one big bee, and I listen to the song of the honeybee.

I am soothed and lulled by this ancient feminine energy. I sit and listen to the hum as it consumes my mind and body. After about thirty minutes, the girls are finished and off they fly in search of something delicious. My body is filled with a sweet richness and a feeling of total contentment—just sitting, being one with the bees, I feel absolutely wonderful. I am full, my body, my mind, my aura all feel complete with a calm peacefulness.

The bees are all around our home now, not just in the backyard, and are out in grand numbers today. We have had a weekend full of people on the land but now it is quiet, and the bees are stirring. The family of hummingbirds has come out to play with them. I am home alone, taking care of the bees and hummingbirds, and all of a sudden there are thousands of honeybees on my back porch. It is a grand visitation; I have never seen so many bees flying together and around me before.

I sit and watch the spectacle. It's as if I had brought all the bees' hives to my back porch and opened them. An expanse that is a good forty feet long and fifteen to twenty feet wide is filled with flying bees. My male basset hound, Baxter, retreats to the house for relief. My female basset hound, Lola, lies on the chair outside. The honeybees land on her head and back as Lola sits without a care in the world.

The honeybees play around us for hours. I watch them fly overhead and dart here and there. They are on my hands, on my drink, and sitting on my clothes. There are honeybees on the table, the couch, and everywhere I look.

This dance of the honeybees is not aggressive at all and they are not batting at my head and face. Instead, they are just having fun. I have no beekeepers' outfit on and I am not working or irritating the honeybees. They have come to dance and sing and I am in awe.

This dance with the honeybees is quite a beautiful love affair of the senses, a dance of love between a beekeeper and the honeybees, as we come together as one.

Eleven

Saying Goodnight

SEPTEMBER

Incredible the lodging but limited by the Guest

Emily Dickinson
1830–1886

I am saying goodnight to the honeybees as fall approaches. This love affair with the little bee is a huge surprise. They are not pets, yet I am in love with this beautiful creature. I feel as close to her as a close friend. Now I understand the relationship the beekeepers in my classes had with their girls and why they spoke about them with such love and affection. This is a new kind of friendship and union gracing my life, with a delicate balance of divine power and beauty. This tiny creature, the honeybee, contains the power to pollinate the world.

The bee and the beekeeper, through time, establish a unique bond. This bond is talked about in many works of prose.

It is a deep relationship, and when the time comes for the end of that relationship there is a ritual called "telling the bees."

The poetic dance between the bee and the beekeeper is described in our myths and tales, and the tradition of telling the bees is ancient. When the beekeeper passes, the queen and her colony of bees must be told. The tale brings forth the feeling of a total cohesive union between the two. If the relationship is not replaced or continued with a new keeper, or the queen and her colony are not told of the beekeeper's passing, the bees will leave or, worse yet, die. So someone must go to the hives and knock three times with a metal key to let the bees know of the passing of their beekeeper and friend.

John Greenleaf Whittier wrote a beautiful poem that speaks of this intricate relationship:

Telling the Bees

Before them, under the garden wall,
Forward and back
Went drearily singing the chore-girl small,
Draping each hive with a shred of black.
Trembling I listened: the summer sun
Had the chill of snow;:
For I knew she was telling the bees of one
Gone on the journey we all must go!

John Greenleaf Whittier
1807-1892

This poem describes the tender and loving union created between the bees and the beekeeper. It is a relationship of equality between a human and a majestic creature of nature. In this relationship there is no ownership instead it is a union of hearts. When the beekeeper is finished with his or her journey, the passing is felt by the bees, and vice versa. I am just beginning to understand this relationship with the bees and it is very old and familiar.

They are now nestled in their hives with the last remaining nectar found from the woods and the fields. I will monitor the hives throughout the fall and winter months as their honey production winds down, making sure they have enough to live on through the cold weather. The queens and their colonies will focus their energy on survival.

My bees are ready for winter and my role is minimal now. I will monitor their water needs and provide feeding supplements for the cold months ahead. That is my primary role until springtime arrives. The honeybees will spend most of their time now inside their dark home creating a warm cocoon for themselves.

Sofia and Rita move into a new stage and so do I. I notice many changes, both within and without. The gardens still have a few flowers and vegetables but most of the beds are prepared for their dormant season. The land's bright colors settle into more calming colors.

The fields have turned a golden rich color with oranges and reds emanating from the vast wheat and cornfields in the distance. The leaves on the trees are also turning their beautiful autumn colors. The leaves fall like raindrops from their perches to create a soft bed on the ground. The bees settle in for winter as well but have left their delicate mark on the entire landscape.

When we bring the intricate pieces together in a cohesive whole something inspiring, beautiful and awesome can come forth. Within the ever-evolving dance, everything touches the dancer. Then the dance changes and everything is touched in turn by the dancer. The individual pieces come together to form something earlier believed inconceivable. The honeybee creates an evolving dance that creates golden nectar—the elixir of the gods. This elixir of honey and mead feeds everything around the bee, creating a circle of life.

I began this journey of beekeeping with the intention of learning about the bee and bringing all the pieces of myself together to create a communion of the whole. My, how this dance with the bees has changed me. I have been given a personal, intricate teaching by the little honeybee this season. I have just begun my journey with this goddess and look forward to continuing the dance.

I hope the honeybee is seen with reverence as information spreads about the beauty she brings to our lives and about the necessity of her gift of pollination to our survival. For myself, I try not to swat anything living because I know that there is perfection in our natural world. These little creatures need advocates for their existence, not their demise.

In spring, my heart dances once again with the honeybee, and I marvel at the many living creatures around me. There are worlds flying around in lilting gaiety. The natural world on our land seems to awaken with the arrival of the honeybee. Insects, animals, flowers, bugs, snakes—everything arrives in multitudes when this little pollinator is present. It is as if the air has changed and a parade has come to life among the community of bees.

The garden and flowers flourish as if they had been attended to for decades. I am in awe of the powers of the little honeybee. It may not be, "lions, tigers, and bears, oh my." No, instead, it is so much more. I sit and marvel and try to take it all in. This absolutely magnificent dance of nature! At first I had trepidation and apprehension of nature, perhaps because it was an unknown to me. In spending time with the natural world I find a great peace and exquisitely changing landscape and it is actually something not to fear at all.

Now, if I listen, I can hear the honeybee calling so sweetly in my ear. I can hear the song of the bees.

The Song of Bees

On a midsummer day the heat rises
Snaking upward in waves that distort the landscape
Until the distance mirrors a mirage
And we lose all sense of what we know.

Seeking solace from the sun we retreat,
find shade beneath an old oak tree
beside a buzzing honey hive,
where we watch the nectar laden ladies struggle in,
weighed down from smelling too many flowers.

As we watch, we cannot help but wonder
what bloom did they feast on today?
Subtle scents to be fanned into honey gold, perhaps?
Or potent, heady brew that will dry down,
molasses brown, thick and pungent?

Standing in the shadow of an ancient canopy
unfurled brand new this spring
we can take a moment to pause,
ponder a life so different from our own,
a life we think we understand,
but can never fully grasp.

Beauty exists in these unknowns-
our imaginations soar with the nubile queen
seeking out the light on her single mating flight,

and though our passions soar with the young queen
we admire her working sisters too,
the countless daughters that will follow soon,
for they remind us that hard work
bears sweetness, liquid gold.

As the summer seeps away,
our oak's lush green canopy changes hue,
slips away leaf by leaf
leaving us to admire aged bark standing stark
against the snow-white fields of winter.

The wind howls cold,
sneaking through chinks and window panes,
but in defiance we spoon into our honeyed gold,
crystallized into creamy smoothness,
nourishing our souls,
as we remember last year's flowers
and our bees

For they are surely ours,
hard toiling ladies
we thank in our hearts
for their delicate confection
and the dream of the all the flowers yet to come.

By Emily Dickinson
1830–1886

Twelve

Delicious Facts

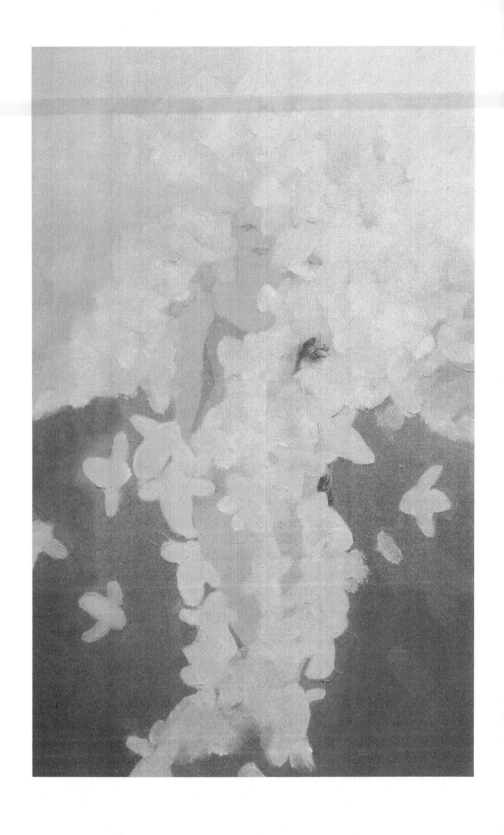

SEPTEMBER

Knowing trees, I understand the meaning of patience.
Knowing grass, I can appreciate persistence.

Hal Borland
1900–1978

Delicious Facts by Ron Post
a Local Beekeeper in the Midwest
and community educator

A honeybee must suckle over two million
flowers to make one pound of honey.
A honeybee travels over fifty-five thousand miles
to create one pound of honey.
An average worker bee makes 1/12 teaspoon of
honey in her lifetime.

A honeybee can fly 15 miles per hour.
It would take about one ounce (or two tablespoons of honey)
to fuel a bee's flight around the world.
A honeycomb cell is a six-sided hexagon.
On average each person consumes about
1.31 pounds of honey per year
A honeybee has four wings.
A honeybee visits about 50 to 100 flowers
during one collection trip.
Honeybees communicate with each other by dancing
and with pheromones or scents.
Honeybees and flowers evolved in the age of dinosaurs.
Bees collect sixty-six pounds of pollen per year, per hive.
The honeybee uses pollen as food.
Pollen is one of the richest and purest natural foods.
Honey is hydroscopic and has antibacterial qualities.
Eating local honey can fend off allergies.
Beeswax is secreted from glands and used by the
honeybee to build honeycombs.
Beeswax is used by humans in drugs, cosmetics,
artists' materials, polish, and candles.
Royal jelly is the powerful milky substance that turns
an ordinary bee into a Queen Bee.

Compiled by Ron Post,
A Bee's Life and More

More Delicious Facts About Bees

There are 25,000 known species of bees.
Each type and species of honeybee performs its waggle dance in a slightly different way.
The queen bee is wholly unable to care for herself. She has attendant bees that follow, feed, and groom her, and also carry her waste away.
Queen bees often make a "piping noise" variously described as sounding like the quacking or tooting noise of a toy trumpet.
The drone or male does not have a stinger.
Honeybees are not native to the United States, the honeybee originated in Europe.

Compiled from *The Beekeeper's Bible*

A Sampling of Some Famous Beekeepers
The Bees Knees at Besthoneysite.com

Aristotle
Peter Fonda
Sir Edmond Hillary
Hippocrates
Sylvia Plath
Martha Stewart
Maria Von Trapp
Steve Val
Brigham Young

Presidents:
Thomas Jefferson
George Washington

More Famous Beekeepers from
4H Beekeeping Club at www.freewebs.com

Pope Urban III
Napoleon Bonaparte
L.L. Langstroth
Sherlock Holmes
Thomas Edison

Two More Famous Beekeepers of Today

Oprah Winfrey

President Barack Obama and First Lady Michelle Obama

As in nature nothing is still, everything is in motion.

Afterword

From the time I began the first adventure into beekeeping I've kept a journal of this extraordinary experience. Before long I had pages upon pages that were the seedlings of this book.

After creating the artwork and completing the first rough draft of my manuscript I came bounding down the stairs with a sense of accomplishment. As I told Daniel about my manuscript I realized he was uneasy. There was a buzzing outside our home. There were hundreds of bees on our front porch and in the bushes and plants. They were everywhere.

I went outside and discovered that bees surrounded the entire house, from the front to back. It had the ominous feeling of Alfred Hitchcock's *The Birds*. Thinking my bees might be swarming, I put my bee suit on and headed to the girls' garden. There, nestled within the garden, were the honeybees. The hives were full. Sofia and Rita were both perfectly content, with attendants flying around them.

For several weeks the massive cloud of bees stayed around our home. They took over the hummingbird feeders and water dishes while the dogs and humans were relegated to the interior of the house. Later, as I was talking with one of my neighbors, I found out that the land behind us was being set up as a bee farm. Over twenty-six hives had been brought in, and this was just the beginning.

The magnificent honeybee has given me a gift. I now have hundreds of honeybees around my home, gardens, and veggies and my caretaking responsibilities have ceased. I stopped adding queens and let the girls join the bee community. Hundreds of bees are always around now, and much like the queen, I feel very well taken care of. There is a nice balance now of bees, hummingbirds, and butterflies around our home.

For you see, the honeybee is in me. I don't need ownership to keep this relationship, and in letting go I received a bounty. I am now a part of this magnificent bee.

Further Reading

1. Chandler, P.J. 2007, *The Barefoot Beekeeper*. Chandler, P.J.

2. Henes, Donna. 2007. *The Queen of My Self*. Monarch Press.

3. O'Donohue, John. 2003, *Beauty: The Invisible Embrace*. Harper Collins.

4. Hubbell, Sue. 1988. *A Book of Bees*. Mariner Books.

5. ABRAMS, 2011, *The Beekeeper's Bible*. Stewart, Tabori & Chang.

6. Eagleman, David. 2011. *Incognito: The Secret Lives of the Brain*. Pantheon Books.

7. Melchizedek, Drunvalo. 2000. *The Ancient Secret of the Flower of Life, Volume 1 and Volume 2*, Light Technology Publishing.

8. Morford, Mark P.O., Robert J. Lenardon. 1995. *Classical Mythology*, Longman Publishers, USA.

9. Post, Ron. 2010. *A Bee's Life and More*. Pamphlet.

10. Crabtree, Maril. 2002. *Sacred Feathers: The Power of One Feather to Change Your Life*. Adams Media Corporation.

11. Abram, David. 1997. *The Spell of the Sensuous: Perception and Language in a More-Than-Human World.* First Vintage Books A Division of Random House, USA.

12. Bonnie Glass-Coffin, Ph.D., don Oscar Miro-Quesada. 2013. *Lessons in Courage*, Rainbow Ridge Books.

13. Magee, Matthew. 2002. *Peruvian Shamanism: The Pachakuti Mesa*, Middle Field Publications.

Appendix

Catalog of Photography

"Honeybee on flower." Orangeaurochs; Sandy, Bedfordshire.

"Honey Bee Macro." Wildxplorer; Karunakar Rayker.

"Artemis of Ephesus." Wikimedia Commons; P. Vasiliadis.

"Crop Circle of Honeybee." lucypringle.co.uk; Lucy Pringle.

"Elaina G Photography." Photography of all original art works by Karrie M. Baxley

Catalog of Artwork
By Karrie Marie Baxley

Karrie Marie Baxley grew up in Dallas, Texas and now calls the Midwest home. She graduated from the University of Missouri with degrees in Business and Computer Information. In 1998 she attended the Westport School of Art and continued her studies at the Kansas City Art Institute majoring in Painting. Karrie Marie is an artist and writer and has shown her work in solo exhibition in Kansas City and art shows across the United States. She also has a piece of work exhibited in the Amazon. She is a Reiki Master, Attunement Practitioner, shaman and medicine woman.

Karrie Marie's work is from the eyes of the feminine embracing the beauty of the human form in communion with our natural world. The creations are from a collage of memories that have paused in time. Bringing forth the communion of experiences and memories with the world we live in.

For further information about Karrie Marie Baxley's work visit KMarieArts.com.